Betrayed by Love
Adored by Lies

A short story anthology

Raynesha Pittman, Kisha Green, Platinum
JoDee Sanders, Fanita Pendleton, Nisha Lanae,
Sha Jones, K.L. Hall, Jevonne, Lette,
Quintessa Turner, Daniele Bigsby & Justin Q Young

TABLE OF CONTENTS

FOOL'S SUPPER
Author Raynesha Pittman

Fuck logical thinking. Hell, the last logical thought. Whitney had went AWOL as the tingling in her toes sent shock waves throughout her body. She couldn't focus long enough now to remember what her last thoughts were about anyways.

"Whose pussy is this?" a deathly hallowed voice asked, but drowning at this depth in pleasure's bottomless pit, she couldn't answer. Hell, she'd be lucky to remember her own damn name, let alone to rack her brain to remember his. The heated sex session; wait, let's call it what it really was – the fuck-a-thon had taken her hostage and consumed her flesh in its entirety. The only sign present that Whitney was still a woman and hadn't endured a metamorphosis to a four-legged bitch in heat was the sweet, musty, lingering scent of her pink abyss in the air.

She never experienced being lost within herself before. It was an uncomfortable, yet addicting feeling she didn't want, but she wouldn't dare allow herself to stop. She couldn't deny the ecstasy of the physical, yet she hated the mental strain it was causing. The stress the tug of war was causing fucked up her mind to the point where she felt like she'd flipped a coin and both sides were victorious in the toss, yet she wasn't the victor of fate's choice. *What is his trifling ass doing to me?* She thought, but as rapidly as her thought formulated, with the same speed it vanished. Her mind was a mile-long tunnel filled with fog. She was sure there was a light that contained all the answers at the end, but her numbness was preventing her from getting to it. There was something causing the fog to become denser, to the point where all she could do was close her eyes and enjoy the exotic bliss.

"Throw that ass back... faster, faster!" the voice demanded and without question, she obliged. It could have been the rhythmic vibes flowing from the bass guitar that played so lovely through her bedroom's speakers, tickling her spine like a feather to the nose doing away with her common sense. Or maybe it was the candle's light dancing on the naked white walls of the bedroom, demanding her attention to the point where she couldn't formulate new thoughts. She considered both possibilities as the flashing patterns of light continued to hypnotize her to the beat of the music playing.

"Oh shit, I'm cummin' again. I swear I hate you!" Whitney yelled out. She felt possessed with the release of fluids as her head began to slowly roll to the left then drag itself to the right.

"No you don't, you love me and this dick!" he corrected.

Damn nicca, you know I do! she yelled in the midst of her mind, not wanting to verbally agree as she continued to rack her brain for the culprit of her absenteeism. She raised the right palm of her hand to her temple and gave it a bump. *Come on, Whitney shit, think. What did Montrell do again?* she silently yelled at herself as he pulled out of her and slapped his hardness across her ass to prevent nutting. Whitney hadn't realized that her thoughts were being ambushed. Of course, the candles and the music played a part in it. That was Montrell's plan. He wanted the combination of Whitney's surroundings, aided by the red satin sheets that caressed her

5

unconcealed curves, to brainwash her. The shit was far from being coincidental.

Nor was the honey that replaced the oil in the bedside burner that he now dripped steadily down her spine as he tossed her salad like only a master chef could. He wanted to create a sexually toxic environment to use as a distraction on her train of thoughts.

"Toot it up in the air." He slapped her ass, making sure to leave his handprint on it when she followed his directions before continuing, "You do what daddy tells you to do, do you understand me?" His plan was working and he knew it because she was too gone in her orgasm to respond. Whenever she came close to remembering why this X-rated boxing match was wrong, the hot stickiness of the drops entwined with his tongue, returned her back to his privately owned land of the lost. Whitney's temporary moment of insanity didn't matter to her anymore, but it should have. All that mattered during her tongue lashing was that she was there. She had arrived at that insane point of love making where pleasure had taken over and the only reality available was the pleasurable psychotic state she found herself trapped in.

She was now unforced and willingly caged in passion's prison, while basking in the company of endless physical satisfaction. She knew she had to be 51/ 50 or being blunt, a damn fool for Montrell's bullshit but she enjoyed every insane second of the shitty situation he trapped her in. He wasn't going to change.

Montrell was and still is her no-good, always cheating, lover with an unwanted title, boyfriend. He had managed to convince her to put up with his bullshit for the past two years. In other words, he had her dick-notized. He was the puppet master and she was the wooden fool hanging from his deceitful strings. The reality of it was sad, but it was the only truth in their relationship. He knew exactly what to do to get her to falsetto the words he wanted to hear. And which mind games he needed to play to control her. There was a time when Whitney would try to fight off his love spell and move on to something better, but Montrell's navigation of her open terrain was too perfect to keep up the fight.

Whitney wasn't one of those weak women who are willing to keep a bad thing going just to say she had somebody. Nor was she one of those low self-esteem having women who depend on validation from others to feel accepted. She wasn't holding on to Montrell for the relationship, because that would be like holding on to shit for the smell. She couldn't let him go because her heart hadn't stopped loving him yet.

In the beginning it was good, like all foundations of a relationships start. Whitney loved everything about Montrell from first sight. It was his looks that caught her attention. The long manicured, black, brown-tipped dreads that fell to the middle of his back and his business causal style of dress had Whitney's nose wide open.

After endless hours of conversation, Montrell's personality made him even more attractive, and the sex between them made her yearn to be his. In hindsight, it was the blend of the three that ultimately caused Whitney to fall in love. Now here they are, two years later and his cheating was pushing her away, leaving Whitney's only reason for keeping this empty relationship was for the sex.

"Yesssssssssssss!" she moaned out, breaking the silence between the two as his tongue tickled her pearl for the umpteenth time.

She knew it wasn't a good reason to stay in the relationship but she was a collector of mind-blowing sex. When it came to collecting sex, Whitney was a connoisseur or an expert, rather than just your

run-of-the-mill ho. Just as those you see visiting vineyard after
vineyard in search of judging and tasting the finest of wines, Whitney
maneuvered the same way. When wine connoisseurs were done
tasting a variety of wines, they purchased the bottle they most
enjoyed. They plan on saving it and drinking it for a special occasion,
or they flaunt their excellent purchase by enjoying a glass with friends.
Although sex and wine are two different scenarios, with Whitney, they
ended the same way. When that last drop has been consumed, the
empty bottle is thrown away and replaced with another; Whitney did
the exact same with her lovers.

She'd date around, sample a few flavors to see what they were
dishing out and keep the best one as her prize. She'd use up her good
thing until it went bad, then throw her lover away and replace them
with someone better. She didn't discriminate and was a full supporter
of the EEOC (Equal Employment Opportunity Commission). Her
present piece is a man, but she did collect women as well. Race, color,
religion, sex, national origin, age, not even a disability will stop her
from giving someone a fair chance at making it to her top shelf.

Once she got a sample of Montrell's style of love making; harsh
yet sensual like the beauty in boxers floating around the ring, she was
hooked. She thought Montrell's style of love making to be a rare find,
so she collected it. The only issue she found with he, is that he didn't
mind sharing his rareness with other connoisseurs. This was against
all Whitney's collector rules. She had been fighting for full ownership
of his pleasing from the beginning and was just about ready to get
one more glass full and throw away the bottle. And he knew it; that's
why he was working so hard to erase her thoughts with love making.

The fight Whitney had put up to get Montrell to take his hands
off of her wasn't working. With every verbal jab she gave, came

Montrell's below the belt punches, outweighing her words. "Tell me the truth, Montrell. You fucked the ugly bitch, didn't you?" Whitney asked, now remembering why she didn't want him touching her. He didn't answer with words; he let his tongue respond by licking her erect clit faster.

"I hate you, Montrell, I swear I do! You're always cheating on me like I don't mean shit to you. Get the fuck off of me!"

"Shut that shit up!" Whitney reached in between her thighs and locked her hands on Montrell's dreads and began lifting his face up with force, but he didn't budge. He knew he had fucked up and although he was tender-headed, he refused to let the pain her grip caused force him to stop.

"You ain't shit, nicca. You can't even hustle right, but you think you can keep playing me and you bring home crumbs. Next time you serve and fuck one of them weed head, Boone's Farm drinking hos of yours, I hope your ass goes to jail." She smacked her lips. "That dick you passing out is garbage anyways, get the fuck off of me, trash man!"

Montrell looked up with a mustache made from Whitney's nicely-trimmed pubic hairs locked on his upper lip. Those words were his pet peeve and Whitney knew it. The majority of his life was spent behind bars because of a bitch screaming those hateful words at him and calling the police seconds later. He'd been arrested for everything known to man over a bitch and swore to never trust one again, but Whitney was different. She had this sassy class about her that only came second to her intelligence. She had degrees and not in medical or nurse assisting, like the majority of bitches he met; they were in accounting. He was digging her, but his dick kept digging into other bitches.

Fool's Supper

She wouldn't believe him if he told so he never bothered to, but meeting her had slowed his rabbit pace down to one mirroring a snail. He used to carry condoms because he always needed them, but now that wasn't the reason why he still kept a magnum hid behind his ID. Montrell held on to it because he didn't want to get caught slipping without one. If there was ever a pussy in need of his pleasing, he wanted to be prepared to handle it in every way possible. That didn't mean he aimed to use it, he just made sure he was always prepared to. If Opening that gold wrapper to fuck his co-worker after promising he'd never cheat on Whitney again, caused Montrell to feel guilty. Otherwise, he would have stopped and sent

Whitney about her way for making the fucked-up remark in regards to his freedom. Instead, he lowered his eyes and said, "Shut up, you know you love this shit!" then continued tongue bathing Whitney's abyss. She started raising hell and began using abusive language. Montrell had her mad and seeing red, but she wanted this sexual boxing match badly. Whitney found herself secretly hoping to lose by a knockout tongue blow in the 10th round. Montrell had fucked up and a TKO wouldn't do it this time. The word "Technical" had no place in this fight, unless it was shortened and changed to technology. He had her so pissed, she was open to any technology that would take his place and increase the frequency and length of the orgasms he caused her to have.

At least, she'd know the machine would be faithful. In the crazy space of Whitney's mind, she thought the more effort Montrell put into pleasing her with all the shit talking she was doing, the sorrier it meant he was. "I hate you, I swear I do. I should have cheated on your ass all those times I had the chance to!"

"No you don't, baby, and you ain't trying to get nobody killed. Stop trying to talk shit and lay your ass back down," Montrell said, now standing over her "Yeah, 1 fucked up again and I'm going to make it up to you. 1 promise!"

He grabbed her by both of her ankles and dragged her to the edge of the bed. When she went to protest, he dug his face back in between Whitney's thighs like his life depended on it. Montrell's tongue imprisoned Whitney's voice somewhere deep within. Once again, causing her to forget what she had to say to him and why she originally protested their love making in the first place.

Her mind was like an impotent man; it kept shooting blanks no matter how hard she tried. The natural sweeteners he used to bring her ecstasy on earth pranced their way up to Whitney's nose and ended their travels on her heavily moistened tongue. For the first time in life, she could taste the air. Her release neared with the sound of the saxophonist's solo blazing through the speakers. The ruffling of the sheets and the squeak from the loose bolt that connected the headboard to the rails wasn't heard. Her labored breathing and the music had muted everything else around it.

The close of round 9 came when the saxophonist reached the peak of her performance. Heavy panting, sweating and the uncontrollable shivering, confirmed round 9 was another victorious round for him. She had never reached heights like this while making love, especially from oral pleasure alone. It was like Montrell had a passport to all of her spots and visited each one repetitively. He wasn't a tourist or a returning visitor to the warm, furry spot that prevented her thighs from joining as one. No, that wasn't the case when it came to him, he was simply returning home. Whitney's body gloved his grasp like chocolate molds to a strawberry at first dip.

Fool's Supper

When the bell sounded in Whitney's head for the start of round 10, she was ready to throw the towel in. Montrell emerged from down under, hovered over her body while moving in between her legs, then rested the right side of his face on Whitney's plump breast. Lifting her legs over his shoulders, he went deep inside of her with three fingers. It wasn't the type of penetration Whitney was craving, but any penetration would be better than none at this point. As she moaned in her soprano voice, Montrell's alto voice joined in, turning her solo into a duet.

Whitney hit a high-pitched, "Ooo yes, baby, YESSS... " He simultaneously hit a low-pitched, Um-hmm baby, I got you..."

Montrell wasn't in the depths of her ocean longer than a minute and she was already shaking like an underwater earthquake, but overflowing more caged than a free-spirited wave of water. It was more like an overdrawn tub with an un-reachable stopper. Not only could she feel the high tide from the tsunami make its way through her, she could also hear it approaching.

"Do you love me, Whit?" Montrell asked quickly, even shortening her name not to waste time.

"You know I love you, Montrell, but you keep fucking..." she managed to respond at the same pace, hoping this newly sparked exchange of words wouldn't ruin her climax. To Montrell, Whitney's audible response meant he wasn't inside of her deep enough. He dug inside of Whitney like an obstetrician checking a dilated cervix, she concluded her sentence by screaming, "Up!" and the song they were singing commenced.

"You ain't going nowhere right, baby?"

Whitney wanted to scream, *shut up, you're killing my mood!* but she knew there was a bigger question coming. Montrell pulled his fingers out of her and replaced it with the 9 inches of fatness he knew she was craving for. He waited for her to answer the question, because Whitney's lips parted and her mouth fell open at the new penetrator. He had a now or never look on his face and with pleasureville just an exit away for Whitney, Montrell rotated his hips so he could get his answer out of her now.

"Yes baby," Whitney said, feeling the electrifying peak on the rise. "Yes." Her heartbeat sped up and sent her boiling hot blood shooting through her veins.

"Then marry me, Whitney, and carry my child."

Montrell didn't give her time to answer, nor did he want Whitney to answer, not at that moment anyways. Once the question rolled off his lips, Whitney's mind was ready to turn back on. He saw it happening and forced himself deeper inside of her. He began moving his body faster and back and forth, while twisting and turning his hips.

Fools Supper

He needed Whitney to be clay in his hands so he could mold her into whatever he wanted her to be. Montrell finally allowed their eyes to meet, knowing Whitney was a sucker for his big hazel eyes. In the dim light, his eyes looked golden against his almond-toned skin. With their eyes now locked, he let the words spill out over his full pear shaped lips.

"Say yes, baby, say you'll marry me." Whitney did exactly as she was instructed; no hesitation involved.

She almost lost the use of her voice as she screamed the word, "Yes." The energy in the moment had taken over her and with power she had no knowledge of having, she flipped them over with her legs, putting herself on top.

"Oh shit, baby, slow down. You gone fuck around and make me nut," he moaned.

"I thought you wanted me to have your baby?" she purred.

"Then say it, say nut in me, daddy. Beg for it!"

"No, you beg for it!" she said as her ride up and down his shaft built momentum. Montrell's eyes tried to lock on the light over the bed as his heartbeat sped up, indicating he was about to nut. Unable to stop the inevitable he yelled out, "Ah shit, I'm nutting; damn that pussy is good, Tiffany... I mean," she cut him off before he could clean up his mistake.

"What the fuck do you mean, Tiffany? You fucking my little sister too?"

To be continued...

IF THIS IS LOVE:
A FLORIDA HOOD LOVE STORY
Author Platinum

Prologue

"How could you do this to me?" Nina yelled as her hot tears streamed down her face. She just couldn't believe her luck. After putting her heart on the line for a man that everyone around her told her wasn't worth it, it was broken.

"Baby, it's not what it seems," Zack huffed. He knew he was caught red handed but wouldn't let his pride down enough to admit it.

"It's not what it seems? I saw the text messages with my own two eyes! You are nothing but a liar and a cheater," Nina screamed. She rushed him, but stopped mid-stride. The closer she got to him, the more pain her heart felt.

"Nina look, what you saw was nothing. I was texting that chick, but I didn't fuck her. It was just for entertainment. Baby, I promise, that's all. Nothing happened," Zack lied. He had to tell her something. That was all he could come up with. He tried to step closer to her, but when he saw her freeze up, he stopped.

"Don't you dare touch me. I hate you. After all, I've done for you and this how you repay me?" Nina roared.

"Nina, I keep telling you, I didn't do anything with that woman. You are the one I love. I promise, baby," Zack begged.

"Nigga, I see your lips moving but nothing's coming out of them but lies. I just can't believe you. You lie for no reason. You lie so much that you start to believe your own lies," Nina huffed.

"I'm not lying, though. This time, I'm telling the truth," Zack said.

"See, there you go again. How long have you been fucking this bitch?" Nina pressed.

"For the last time, I did not fuck her. I was only talking to her," Zack clarified.

"Fucking! Talking! It's all the fucking same in your head. How fucking long?" Nina repeated. "Not that..." Zack started, but stopped when Nina held up her hand.

"If you lie, so help me God, I will fuck you up where you stand," Nina fumed.

"Look, you want the truth so I'm going to tell you, but you got to promise me you won't get mad," Zack suggested.

"Too muthafucking late, nigga. I'm past mad, now get to talking," Nina taunted.

"Alright, I started talking to her about three months ago, but with never met up or anything like that. We were just texting every now and then," Zack blurted.

"Where you meet this bitch at?" Nina let her next question roll off her tongue with the quickness. "I met her at McDonald's that night you sent me there to grab you something to eat," Zack mumbled.

"So in these messages, you asked her when can you come fuck her again, so when was the first time you fucked her?" Nina argued.

"That's the thing, I didn't. I was just trying to get some head from her, that's it," Zack admitted.

"Get your shit out my house and lose my muthafucking number," Nina told him.

"Baby, you don't mean that. You are just mad at me right now, but this will all die down soon. I will prove to you that this time, I didn't do anything," Zack said.

"Don't tell me what I mean. I know I don't want you. You just nasty. Out in these streets fucking God knows who or what. I be damned if I let you bring me anything back that I can't get rid of," Nina hissed.

"Nina, baby, I'm not out there fucking nobody. All I want is you. I only want to be with you," Zack expressed.

"Liar! You are nothing but a liar. If you wanted only me you would be entertaining another bitch!" Nina ranted.

"Ok, look. I know I'm wrong for talking to other women, but I don't fuck 'em so that means I'm not cheating on you. Baby, just stop all this. You know I love you." Zack eased towards her. He wrapped his arms around her neck, pulling her close to him. He felt bad for the way he had hurt her.

"Zack, I love you too, and that's why we are over. I can't keep letting you dog me out and have me out here looking like a fool. I'm going to Niya's house where I will stay for the night, but when I return tomorrow, I want you gone." Nina reached up and gave him a peck on his cheek and made her exit. She was broken. The more she looked at him, the more her heart hurt. He was the man she thought she would marry and have kids with, but so much had happened within the short period of time they had been together, that she had had enough.

All This Love: A Florida Hood Story

Zack stood in the middle of their bedroom and just looked around. He couldn't believe he had let a strong, black, hard-working woman get away because of his mistakes. He took a seat on the edge of their king size bed and placed his head in the palm of his hands. He let Nina's words run through his head over and over again. With nowhere to go, Zack had to give the only person he knew would let him crash on their couch, until he could come up with somewhere to live.

Zack pulled out his cell phone, looking at the screen saver and just smiled. It was a picture of him and Nina at the Crab Shack hugged up. He let flashes of how happy they were flip through his head. He could remember that night just like it was yesterday. That was the night he knew he fell in love with her. Zack snapped out of his thoughts and continued to dial a number. He placed the phone to his ear. He waited for someone to answer.

"Baby, please don't hang up. I promise to never..." Zack stopped mid-sentence at the sound of the dial tone in his ear.

Nina didn't want to hear any more of his broken promises and his lies. Hanging up on him was the nicest thing she could do. She scrolled through her phone in her contacts. She came to his number and pressed the button "Put Number on Block List". There was nothing else they had to talk about. She then placed her phone on the passenger seat of her car and continued driving. Time and space were what she needed and she was about to get just that. She knew Zack would do a pop-up at Niya's house, looking for her as he always did when they broke up. His hunch would fail this time because her plan was not to go to Niya's house. She looked up at the sign that read I-75 North left lane. Nina flipped on her turn signal and got over in the left lane. She was trying to get as far away from Bradenton as she possibly could.

Platinum

CHAPTER 1

Nina let the wind blow through her hair as she cruised down the street. Life was good for her. She had just moved back home to be close to her family. Now her only problem was to find somewhere to call home. Living with her family wasn't an option. Nina had been single for over three years, after her last relationship went south. She turned the corner and saw two dudes walking down the street. She swerved over to go around them and kept riding.

"Nina!" someone hollered her name. She looks in her rearview mirror and noticed her homie walking. Hitting the brakes and putting her car in reverse, she backed up to him.

"What the fuck do you want?" Nina smirked.

"Damn dawg, it's like that?" The dude laughed.

"Man, I don't have time for your shit today. I got shit to do," Nina huffed.

"Well damn, nigga, can you just give us a ride?" Jamal added.

"Where y'all going?" Nina asked, still talking to him through the window.

She looked behind him at the other dude, who was just standing there smiling at her. "I need you to take me to the store and then just drop us off at our room," Jamal instructed.

"C'mon nigga, damn," Nina unlocked the car doors. "And what the fuck are you standing back there just smiling for?"

"My nigga high as fuck right now. He done smoked some of that gas," Jamal explained.

"Man, I can talk for myself," the dude spoke up. "I'm smiling because I've been looking for you."

"I don't know what the fuck for, ain't you married or some shit?" Nina laughed.

"Yeah but I'm finna get a divorce, so what's up?" the dude got straight to his point.

"Nothing but the sky, nigga. The fuck you mean?" Nina couldn't do nothing but laugh. *The nerve of some men.* She knew she had been off the dating scene for a while, but knew for sure that's not how things were supposed to go.

"Man, stop flagging on my nigga. You know he been wanted to holla at you for a minute," Jamal added his two cents.

"Boy, stop playing. Zack ain't checking for me and I'm sure as hell not checking for him. Now where y'all going, so I can finish looking for somewhere for me to stay," Nina brushed them both off.

"Yo, your stank ass don't have to act like that. My nigga was just trying to holla," Jamal joked.

"Fuck you, nigga. You always got something smart to say. Where the hell you going so I can hurry up and get you out my damn car?" Nina asked.

She loved to talk major shit. Being the woman she was, she wouldn't let anyone say anything out the way to her, without talking shit back.

"Take me to the store by Popeyes, heffa," Jamal replied.

"Fuck you, bastard," Nina responded, while heading in that direction. She didn't hear a peep out of Zack. She knew he liked her, but wasn't ready for another relationship. Nina pulled up in front of the store. Jamal hopped out the car while still talking shit, but Nina didn't respond. She put the car in park and pulled out her cell phone. She pulled up her Facebook app while ignoring Zack, who was just looking out the window.

"Aye man, you already know a brotha been trying to get atcha for a minute. What's it going to take for me to take you out on a date?" Zack broke the silence.

Nina thought before she answered. She didn't want to come off as a bitch, so she chose her words wisely.

"Look, Zack; you ah nice dude and all, but I don't think I'm ready for another relationship right now. Plus, you already have too much on your plate with your wife and all." Nina looked back at him. By the look on her face, he could tell she was being funny but chose to let it go.

"Trust me; I can handle everything you throw this way. My soon to be ex-wife won't be a problem," Zack admitted.

"Yeah, yeah, yeah, we will see." Nina shrugged.

"I like a feisty woman. All that shit you talking, turning a brotha on," Zack smirked.

"Call it whatever you want to, but I bet I can back my shit up. This ain't what you want," Nina chuckled. She liked the little bit of attention he was giving her. She knew she wasn't a bad-looking woman. She was light-skinned, stood about 5' 7" and was thick in all the right places.

"Show me better than you can tell me then," Zack pressed. Nina was just about to respond, but Jamal got back in the car so she just smiled.

"What the fuck that nigga said to you that got you smiling and shit?" Jamal jumped right in on her. "Stay out of grown folk's business, lil boy. Now, where am I dropping your ass off at?" Nina switched up on him.

"Take me to my damn room. Damn, your ass act like you hard of hearing," Jamal laughed. He loved trying to get up under her skin. The two had known each other for over ten years and were more like brothers and sisters.

"I can't stand your Creaser looking ass," Nina called him out his name.

"That's alrite I know somebody who likes it," Jamal stuck his tongue out at her. Everyone in the car busted out laughing. Jamal was a clown. He would keep you laughing none stop.

"Don't nobody like that shit wit yo ugly ass," Nina laughed.

She pulled in front of Jamal's room and didn't even pull into a parking space. She wanted to make it clear she wasn't staying for any reason at all.

"Yo muthafucking friend likes it. Hell, I know she loves ah nigga. Look how long we been together," Jamal assured.

"What the fuck ever. Just get the fuck out so I can go," Nina demanded.

"Man, park this muthafucking car and come upstairs and smoke with ah nigga. Your dumb ass just got back in town, now you want to act all brand new," Jamal told her.

"I don't have time to smoke. I done already told you; I need to be house searching and don't have time to just be sitting around smoking all day," Nina hollered.

"Shut the hell up. You think you slick, you just trying to get away from my brother," Jamal busted her. She was trying to leave just as fast as she came. It was something about Zack she liked, but wasn't sure if she was ready to take on all his baggage he was carrying.

"Boy, I do got shit to do. Ain't nobody worried about you or him; now get the fuck out," Nina repeated.

"I ain't going nowhere until you park this bitch," Jamal declared.

All This Love: A Florida Hood Story

"Looks like y'all finna be going with me, because I'm not parking or even going up them stairs, for that matter," Nina finalized.

Jamal mushed her upside the head and then jumped out the car. Zack soon followed and Nina pulled off without another word.

CHAPTER 2

Nina stopped by her friend Niya's house one day and the first face she saw was Zack's, sitting on the porch. She tried to walk past him without saying anything to him, but he wouldn't let that happen. "Oh, you just going to walk past me like you don't see me sitting here?" Zack muttered, trying to block her path to the door.

"Boy, move out my way. I see you, but that don't mean I have to speak to you." Nina shoved him. She quickly walked in the door without even knocking. She and Niya had been friends for over ten years. They were more like sisters with different mothers.

"Sister! What are you doing?" Nina sang, making her presence known.

"I'm in the kitchen," Niya yelled.

Nina walked in towards the kitchen to see her friend. She had been missing her for a while. They hadn't hung out for over a year.

"Damn bitch, it smells good in here," Nina told her.

"You know I be doing what I can do, when I do it," Niya laughed.

"Whatcha cooking?" Nina asked, taking a seat at the kitchen table.

"Nothing much but some cabbage, mac and cheese, cornbread, and fried chicken," Niya answered.

"Bitch, I need my plate," Nina told her.

Nina was a lil thick and loved to eat. Hel, eating was a hobby for her.

"After my nigga eats," Niya said.

"Fuck him. I can't stand his ass. Always talking shit. Where his stupid ass at anyway?" Nina asked. "He ain't out that door?" Niya replied.

"Nah, I didn't see him when I came up," Nina stated.

"I'ma kick his ass. He didn't tell me he was going nowhere," Niya threatened.

"Well, he sure ain't out there," Nina added. She liked to see her friend show out on Jamal. It was the funniest thing in the world to her.

"Is Zack out there?" Niya pressed.

"Yeah, he is. He was sitting on the porch when I came in," Nina admitted.

"Oh hell, that means Jamal's ass ain't too far then. He must have walked to the store," Niya responded. "So what the fuck is really going on? Jamal told me about Zack liking you."

"Nothing, hell; we all know that nigga likes me but sista, he got too much baggage. I don't have the time or the patience to deal with another married man," Nina informed her.

"Well, one thing I do know is, he is finna get a divorce from his wife. That's why he is down here. She put his ass out and he was living on the streets for a minute until he came here," Niya explained. Both ladies walked into the front room to finish their conversation. Nina knew Niya wouldn't lie to her, so the wheels in her head were turning. She had to admit that Zack was very attractive and she always had a soft spot for him.

"Well, that may be the case, but I don't know about that," Nina sighed.

"Bitch, ain't nobody telling you to marry the nigga. Just let him take you on a date and then see where it goes," Niya hollered.

They both busted out laughing.

"Girl, I don't think I'm ready for all that right now. You know I ain't been out on a date in over three years," Nina smirked.

"That's why your ass is going on that date. Hell I know you got cobwebs growing down there by now," Niya joked and they erupted in laughter once again. Too busy laughing, they never noticed Jamal and Zack had walked in the room.

"What the hell's so funny?" Jamal asked.

"None of your damn business, nigga. Always in somebody else's business. If you get your muthafucking own, then you won't have the need to be in ours. How about this, how about you spend six months out the year minding your own damn business, and spend the other six months staying out other people's business? How about that shit?" Nina snapped.

"Shut the hell up. I wasn't talking about your gray teeth ass. I was talking to my baby," Jamal said before he placed a kiss on Niya's lips.

"Baby, is the food done?" Jamal changed the subject.

"It will be in a few, but I was just talking to Nina about us all going out one night. Like a double-date or something," Niya suggested.

"Hell nah, I'm ain't going nowhere with her ass. Y'all can go," Jamal protested.

"Fuck you. I don't want to go anywhere with your stank ass either." Nina pushed his head. The two begin to play fight and Nina rushed him. He fell back on the bed screaming. Nina had him pinned up on the bed.

"Ugh! Get her off me. Damn baby, you just going to let her do me like that?" Jamal hollered.

"I don't have anything to do with that," Niya uttered.

"Y'all play too much," Zack whispered.

"You just hush up, 'cause you don't want none of this either," Nina huffed, taking her seat on the couch in the corner of the room. She was out of breath from years of smoking Newport's.

All This Love: A Florida Hood Story

"So what y'all going to do? Y'all going to take us out on a date or what?" Niya changed the subject.

"Man...Niya, your friend or should I say sister, don't want to go out on a date with me," Zack protested.

"I wouldn't take her ass nowhere anyways, brah. You know all she going to do is talk shit," Jamal told him, while firing up the blunt.

"I keep telling you to shut the hell up. I don't give ah fuck. I don't want to go anywhere with y'all anyways. Sister, I'm finna get up out of here before I catch a charge. Call me later," Nina said, before she made her exit.

"Ok girl, I will," Niya laughed. She was used to her best friend and her man arguing all the time. It seems to her that Jamal couldn't function without picking an argument with somebody in their circle.

"Call me when the food is done." Nina poked her head back in the door with a smile.

"Yo greedy ass always wants something to eat. Yo ain't getting shit from over here," Jamal screamed.

Nina just slammed the door without responding. She hated the way she would let Jamal get up under her skin. They had been fighting like sisters and brothers for years and it was starting to annoy her. She didn't respond because she already knew her friend was going to fix her a plate and also bring it to her. That's how their friendship was set up. They both did things for each other and made sure they both were straight.

CHAPTER 3

It had been over a month since Nina had seen or talked to Zack. She did talk to Niya, however, who told her Zack was asking about her every chance he got. With trying to find a place to live and finding a good-paying job, Nina still didn't want anything to do with him. She believed that a man and a woman shouldn't start a relationship until they were both stable and had no loose ends as far as other girl or boyfriends. She was now thirty-four years old and had lived enough to know she was ready to settle down with a man who would love only her.

Nina had a child to protect and wasn't for meanless relationships. She wasn't sure Zack was ready for the kind of relationship she was ready for. She was looking for someone she could grow with and get old with. She loved her son with all her heart, but was still bitter at how her relationship ended with his father. They had been in a relationship for over four years. When she met Toby, he was legally separated from his wife. Nina wasn't too happy to learn that he was married, but after finding out that he was legally separated from his wife for over ten years, she accepted it. She became pregnant with his fourth child.

Nina felt that everyone around her was happy for her and thought she would marry Toby. He had moved in with her right after the baby was born. The one thing Nina loved about Toby was he wasn't a drug dealer. He had a nine to five and didn't indulge in drugs either. She was okay with how their relationship was progressing, up until the day she popped the big question. She begins to think about that dreadful day.

All This Love: A Florida Hood Story

"Bae, I got a question for you," Nina cooed, walking into their bedroom.

Toby was in the bathtub, taking a sit-down bath in their Jacuzzi tub. "Yeah baby, I'm in here," Toby yelled.

Nina walked in the bathroom and a naughty smile spread across her face. She began to undress herself, wanting to join him. Their bathtub was the best place to have sex. Nina loved when Toby would bend her over the side of the tub and beat her pussy up. She eased down in the water, straddling him. He wrapped his arms around her neck and pulled her in for a long passionate kiss.

"Damn, that was good," Toby smiled. He had to admit he loved the hell out of Nina.

"I got something else for you," Nina sang.

"I thought you had something to ask..." Toby stopped mid-sentence at the feel of Nina's tightness wrapped around his manhood.

"Damn it!" Toby groaned in her ear.

"You like this pussy, daddy?" Nina asked, making her ass jump up and down on his nine-inch rod. The two couldn't hold their excitement and began to splash water all over the floor. Nina rode him like a stallion. She could feel her orgasm building in the pit of her stomach.

"Oh baby, I'm finna cum," Nina screamed.

Toby wasn't ready for her to cum just yet. He stood up in the bathtub while still holding on to her. He still had his dick deep inside her guts as he bent down to let the water out. Nina was so horny she couldn't help herself; she began to contract her pussy muscles around him, pulling him in deeper. Toby's knees became weak at the sensation she was sending through his body. He placed both of her feet on the floor of the tub, releasing himself from inside of her.

Toby forcefully pushed Nina up against the wall, placing kisses all over her neck. Nina moaned out in pleasure. He trailed kisses all the way down to her honey pot. He spread her legs and propped one up on the side of the tub. He had full access to her clit.

He then blew on it with his warm breath and that sent chills up and down Nina's spine. She began to pull at his head to put it in the place she wanted it to be. Toby devoured her clit like it was his last meal. Nina couldn't take much more.

"Oh baby, I'm cumming. Tobyyyy, I'm cumminnnggg," Nina screamed.

"Cum for daddy, baby," Toby muttered, in between slurps. He sucked up all her juices as he fought against her protests. He pinned both of her hands behind her head and ate her pussy just the way he wanted too.

"Baby, no stop; I can't take anymore," Nina whined. She had tears rolling down her cheeks as she tried to close her legs.

"Tell me who pussy this is." Toby wouldn't let up. He knew just what he was doing. He loved the way she tasted.

"It'ssss yours. Baby, it's yourrrs," Nina hollered.

Toby released her, but not before he spun her around. He bent her over and slides his rod back inside of her. He banged her back out until he brought both of them to an orgasm. Nina was out of breath and couldn't move. She had to give it to Toby; he never left her unsatisfied. The two got out of the tub and joined one another in the bed, where they sexed each other for the rest of the day.

Nina heard a car horn and was brought out of her thoughts. Toby was the love of her life, but he had left a bad taste in her mouth. They way they broke up was too much for her to let another man get too close to her heart. She pulled off and made a left turn on Bee Ridge, heading to work. Nina had found a job working as a CNA at an assisted living facility. She loved helping other as much as she loved living. She pulled up in front of her new job and killed the engine. She bowed her head and said a quick prayer as she always did, before she planted her feet safely on the pavement. She grabbed her purse and closed the door. As she began walking into the building, her phone began to ring. She looks down at the number and quickly pressed end.

"Why the fuck is he calling me this early?" Nina huffed out loud as she reached for the door handle. Toby had been calling her more lately and she refused to answer his calls. She was over the way he left her, but didn't see any reason for them to hold a conversation with each other. Things were going well in her life and she didn't need him coming back in to mess up her thoughts and actions

CHAPTER 4

Nina had just got off work. She worked another sixteen-hour shift and was dog tired. Her feet throbbed from standing on them all that day. It was days like this that she regrets not having a man. She walked to her car quickly and hopped in. After starting it up, she pulled off into traffic. Heading to her hotel room so she could get some much-needed rest was what she had planned to do. It took her forty-five minutes to get to her room.

She was thankful Toby took her son in while she was still trying to get on her feet. She thought maybe she would give him a call back to make sure her son was okay. Nina slid her key card in the door to gain access to her room. The first thing she did was kicked off her shoes and dropped her things in the chair by the door. She looked around her room and made a mental reminder that she needed to do a deep cleaning. She walked into the bathroom and flipped on the light. Taking a look in the mirror, Nina could see her eyes had bags up under them. Sleep was something she didn't get much of. Nina turned on the shower water and began to remove her clothes.

She jumped into the shower without a second guess. Working with older people was a job you had to love. It was very challenging and hard work. Nina had been doing nursing work for years. She'd started with her first summer job.

After finding out that there were a lot of people out there in the world, who didn't have much family or no family at all that cared about them once they were placed into a home, Nina couldn't stop trying to be there for them. She could hear her cell phone going off, but let the call go to the voicemail. She refused to get out of her shower. The hot water was massaging her aching bones. She stayed in the shower for thirty more minutes before she got out.

Nina dried her body with one towel and then wrapped a dry one around herself. She felt it was no need to put on clothes; it was only her in the room. She walked in the room and retrieved her purse. Grabbing her phone, she looked at her missed calls. She had one from Toby again and another one from her friend, Niya.

Nina let her mind drift back to the day she felt it in her bones that it was over with her a Toby.

Nina and Toby were sitting in their living room enjoying their Sunday dinner while watching the football game. She was a San Francisco 49ers fan and he liked the Dallas Cowboys. When the commercial came on, Nina began to ask him questions. "Bae, when are you planning on getting your divorce from your wife?" Nina spoke up out the blue.

"Where'd that come from?" Toby shrieked.

"I've been thinking on it hard lately. I just don't want to continue to date someone else's husband. I want my own," Nina explained to him.

"Nina, I've told you already that I can't afford to get a divorce right now from my wife. Things between us are good, so let's just continue to live our life as we are," Toby told her.

"Toby, you told me that same lie three years ago. I'm starting to think you are never going to divorce her," Nina fumed. She hopped up off the couch and took her plate in the kitchen. The more he made excuses for not wanting to divorce his wife, the more she felt like their whole relationship was a lie.

"Damn, Nina; you know what I'm up against. I'm already paying child support for my other kids and I have my daughter on my

insurance at work, so I can't divorce her until my daughter graduates high school," Toby stated.

"You have lost your mind if you think we are going to keep shacking up together for another two years while you are married. You got me all the way fucked up," Nina finalized. She walked away from him, because she knew it was going to be another argument.

"How I got you fucked up? You knew I was still married to her when we first got together; I don't see why it's a problem now," Toby yelled.

"It's a muthafucking problem now, because we been together for over three years and you still haven't divorced her yet. I'm sick of playing the other fucking woman," Nina hollered.

"How are you just the other fucking woman? You are my only woman. You know my wife and I have nothing to do with each other. We are just married on paper for my kids. That's it. You tripping about the wrong muthafucking thing if you ask me," Toby screamed.

"Nah, I'm not tripping about nothing. I'm telling you now that I'm not going to continue in the relationship, being just your damn baby momma. Fuck that shit you talking about," Nina hissed.

"Woman, you are crazy. How you go from my ole lady to just my baby momma? For the last time, I'm going to tell you this; my divorce will get filed when I get the money to file it, when my daughter graduates from high school, and when I get damn well ready to. I'm not going to let you force me into this," Toby told her, turning on his heels.

Nina was furious and spent the rest of the night in her bedroom alone. That was the day their relationship took a turn for the worst. It was downhill from there.

Nina was brought back from her thoughts with her cell phone ringing. She looked down at the phone and "Fuck Boy" popped up on her screen. It was Toby. She took a deep breath before she slid her finger across the screen to answer it."Hello," Nina huffed.

"Well damn; I'm glad you're not dead and you're okay," Toby sarcastically said."What could you possibly want?" Nina asked with much attitude.

It didn't help much that she had just finished thinking about him. She didn't know why her thoughts were on him more lately, but they were and she didn't know how to deal with it. "I do have our son. You can call every once in a while to at least check up on him," Toby said.

"I've been working long hours and was going to call him tomorrow on my day off. I just got done working sixty-seven hours this week alone, Toby, give me a fucking break," Nina sighed. She stood up from her bed and walked to the dresser which looked like a mini-bar. She had everything from wine to beer to liquor. Pulling her Malibu close to her, she didn't waste any time putting the bottle to her lips and taking a big swig.

"Look, I don't need your attitude right now. Your son has been asking about you, so that is why I was calling you. It won't hurt you to pick up the phone and just call him," Toby hissed.

"Now you see what I had to go through for the last two years alone. It damn sure must have hurt you, because we never heard from you unless you were trying to get back between these legs," Nina screamed.

"Don't flatter yourself. I only called you twice on that tip, but it didn't happen again after you stood a brother up the last time," Toby said.

"Yep, you damn right I stood you up, because I think it's really disrespectful for you to be calling me about some pussy instead of your son!" Nina yelled.

"Yeah, yeah, yeah, I get it and trust me; it won't happen again. Now when are you coming to get him? Ain't school about to start down there?" Toby questioned.

"Damn, you only had him a month and already bitching about when I'm going to come get him. You can bring him home tomorrow if you like. It won't change a damn thing; you'll still be a sorry ass nigga." Nina hung up her phone in his face.

She was done playing his game. It never failed, if Toby got something over her head he always harassed her and she was sick of it.

To be continued...

TWO TRUTHS AND A LIE
Author K.L. Hall

Chantel Love

When I was a little girl, I prided myself on getting a good education, saying my prayers at night and grace before each and every meal, and most importantly, someday finding a man I could build my future with, the king to my queendom if you will. My king was Terrence Cordell Love.

Have you ever known what it feels like to love somebody to death? That's how I felt about Terrence. He was everything to me. We were so in tune with one another, if he were to get shot, I would feel the bullet pierce through my skin and bleed. We were one, you hear me? One being. One entity. One everything. However, don't get me wrong, Terrence Love was no saint. No indeed. In fact, he was far from it...

February 14, 2017

I laid awake that night, unsettled and battling with the insomnia of my emotions. Terrence was lying next to me with his back turned, sleeping peacefully like a newborn baby. I turned my head to stare at his back and that's when I heard the muffled vibration from the iPhone tucked deep inside his pants pocket. Knowing it was well after one in the morning, I rolled my eyes.

This nigga must think I'm stupid, I thought. Being the proud nosey female that I am, I crept out of bed, grabbed his True Religion jeans and made my way into the bathroom adjacent to our master bedroom. As soon as I locked the door, I sat on the toilet and dug in his pockets. His phone was vibrating consistently like a washing machine. I closed my eyes and took a deep breath before looking at the screen. *Nah, fuck this*, I thought as I dug into his other pocket. "Bingo," I whispered, as I pulled out a freshly rolled blunt and red BIC lighter.

I put the blunt up to my lips and sparked the flame, inhaling slowly. My nerves were jumping around my body like frogs and I needed something to calm me down. Once the smoke filled my lungs, I could instantly feel my body start to relax. Although I wasn't ready to face the truth, it was time for me to find out exactly what Terrence had been hiding from me. I pulled the smoke into my lungs once more as my eyes darted from right to left across the screen. I sat there, rereading the text messages between him and an unsaved number repeatedly as the pain vibrated my chest.

How could he? I thought as I looked down at my ring finger. You see, there was no ring on it, but Terrence and I had agreed that jewelry was for show and wouldn't solidify the bond between us, so instead of visiting Jacob the Jeweler, we visited Travis at the nearby tattoo shop and carved each other's initials into the skin of our ring fingers. I thought it was romantic at the time. Terrence made me feel like everything we did was something new and exciting that no other couple had ever done before.

That was six months ago. In this moment, I felt like the stupidest woman on earth. Most women could pawn a ring or even flush it down the toilet, but every time I caught a glimpse of my hand, I would be reminded of him. It would be a constant reminder of his infidelity and his lies, branded on my skin.

I shook my head and continued to read the messages that were tearing me apart word by word. By the looks of it, he'd been conversing with that unsaved number for weeks, maybe even longer. He was reciting the same words to some bitch as if she held the same clout as me, *his wife*, as if he was an actor in a movie. That's when I realized our entire three-year relationship was a facade. It was all pretend. Maybe I never had him. Maybe I never would.

When Terrence and I first met, it was magical, for me at least. I got pregnant after only having sex with him a few times. I should've known better back then, but I didn't. All the signs were there. He had two other baby mamas, who each swore they were the apple of his eye. He was still in a "relationship" with the second baby mother, Veronica, when he got with me. She hated my guts back then and she still does. I bet she would have laughed right in my face if she saw me then. Serves me right, I guess.

Anyway, for years, I'd been a sucker for him; turning a blind eye to his infidelity and his lies. I guess if you can't turn a hoe into a housewife, you can't turn a fuckboy into a good husband either. Now, before you start judging and pointing the finger, hear me out. I only stayed with him because of our son, Akeem. I didn't want him to be a statistic. You know, another black boy growing up without knowing what it was like to have a full-time father around.

I didn't want to be just another one of Terrence's "baby mothers" either, but if the shit didn't work, it didn't work. I smeared my tears and mascara against the back of my hand as I read the words that made my heart stop.

"I love you too, and I can't wait for our prince to be born."

I never knew what it felt like to die until that very moment. I had died a thousand deaths by just reading fourteen words. There I was, thinking things were going fine, while he had plans to run off and start a new life with a bitch he didn't even care enough about to save her number in his phone. Or was it me and our son that he didn't care about? Or his other two children? At that moment, I didn't know.

I didn't know if any of it mattered either. I had so much hope for the two of us, but in the blink of an eye, it had all disappeared.

I stared at myself in the mirror, but all I could see were the text messages looking back at me. My thoughts were consumed by the words he'd sent to some other bitch. The bitch who thought that she was going to get my husband and take my family away from me. The bitch who thought that she was going to easily rip my heart out of my chest and I would give up breathing just like that. No. Hell no. Fuck no! I loved him. He was mine. He was always going to be mine until death did us part.

Terrence was my king, but I never knew I had placed him on a pedestal until he was too high for me to reach. So high up that he could walk all over me and disregard our vows whenever he saw fit to scratch an itch. I'm even ashamed to say that at times, I worshipped him like a false idol. It was the good things that kept me in line, you know? From his kisses to his touch, to the family photos of the three of us, hanging up high in frames like my most prized possession.

Remember when you were a kid and all you wanted to do was smile, laugh, play and be loved? That's because when you're young, adults teach you about how it's the right thing to do to be good to people, to spread love and to be kind. But what happens when you've done all you can and you don't get the same thing in return? The more time I spent in the bathroom, the closer I came to the revelation of my bittersweet love story.

When I needed comfort, he gave me dick. When I needed reassurance, he gave me blank stares and excuses. When I needed love, he gave me sugarcoated lies. That's when I realized that my love was never enough to make him want to step down from that pedestal. My love was never enough to break him out of the fuckboy mentality he'd Etch A Sketched in his brain.

My love was never enough for him, because my love was never enough for me. I didn't love myself enough to know when enough was enough, or that the cat and mouse game shit was for suckers. With Terrence, I knew I couldn't just go out and fuck his homeboy or have a random one-night stand with another man. That wouldn't be enough. I longed for the sympathy that I knew I was never going to get. But I knew what I would get. *Revenge.*

That was the only thing that would get him the fuck out of my system for good. Just that hint of satisfaction in my most desperate and vulnerable hour made me snap. I hit the blunt one last time, then ashed it and put it out in the sink.

My eyes were bloodshot red and puffy. I splashed some water on my face, closed my eyes and prayed to God for forgiveness for what I was about to do. "Amen," I mumbled, and then turned on my heels to walk out of the bathroom with his phone in the pocket of my sweatpants.

I swung the door open and let the smoke that packed the bathroom, filter into the bedroom. The fresh air was cool against my skin. I looked over at him with disgust written all over my face. Forgiveness was a hard pill to swallow and I was gagging. I walked out of our bedroom and down the hall into our son's room. He was an angel, but not even he could take away the amount of pain and rage boiling inside me. I walked over to the side of his bed and bent down to kiss his forehead.

"Mommy loves you, Akeem," I whispered in his ear and then gently closed the bedroom door behind me. I stood in the hallway, staring at the doorframe to our bedroom, frozen in my step for a few seconds. Possibly contemplating, reconsidering the extent of my premeditated actions even. The longer I stood, the more I could feel the watered seed of doubt blossoming in the back of my mind. *It's now or never. He hurt you, Chan. Are you really going to let him get away with what he did to you? He got you out here looking crazy. He's playing you! You need to show him what's up!*

Payback is a bitch; I heard all the voices scream to me inside my head. Nevertheless, I walked back into our bedroom and opened his nightstand drawer. His silver pistol was buried underneath old receipts and other knickknacks that were just taking up space. I slowly pulled it out of the drawer and held it in my hand, getting used to the weight. I'd held a gun plenty of times before, but never that one. His pistol, or the 'Silver Bullet' as he called it, was his favorite piece.

"Wake up, Terrence," I said, pointing the gun to his back.

"What?" he mumbled, still half asleep.

"I said wake up! What is this, huh?" I asked, holding up his cell phone in my other hand He took one look at me before I threw it at him, hitting him in the side of the head. He groaned in pain. "Yo, Chan, what the fuck is your problem?" he yelled, gripping the side of his head.

"You know exactly what my problem is! How could you cheat on me and get a bitch pregnant, T?"

"What are you talking about?" he asked.

"Stop playing dumb and be man enough to own up to your shit! It's right there in black and white!"

"Just hold up a second and put my gun down! What are you even doing with that shit, huh? You gon' shoot me? Over some bitch?" he yelled.

Two Truths And A Lie

I slowly turned my head from left to right, cracking my neck. I could feel beads of sweat populating on my forehead and in the palm of my hand. My index finger was wrapped around the trigger like wrapping paper on a birthday present. I slowly backed away from him and flipped on the bedroom light. Our eyes landed right on each other's. I searched his eyes for a trace of me, but all I could see was fear. I guess maybe if I would've seen remorse, repentance or even sorrow, it would've halted me. Stopped me dead in my tracks, you know? But his fear...that just fueled me.

"Why? Wasn't I good to you? Huh? What did I do to deserve this? I married you! Even with the two babies and all the fucking baby mama drama, I fucking agreed before God to love and cherish you for the rest of my life! Look at what you've done to me! I'm a fucking mess and it's all because of you!" I screamed.

"Look, Chan. I fucked up, a'ight? I can't change the present situation, I'm not a magician...but baby please, please just put the gun down. Let's just talk about it. We can figure this out, together," he pleaded, trying to reason with me. "Didn't anybody ever tell you, you can't reason with a crazy person?"

"You're not crazy, baby. I don't think you're crazy. You're just hurt and I get that. That's on me," he said, pointing to his chest.

I scoffed. "Oh, now you *don't* think I'm crazy? That's not what you were saying to that bitch!" Terrence sighed, knowing he couldn't lie his way out of the tangled web he'd woven for himself.

"You're right. I shouldn't have said that." He nodded.

"I never wanted to do anything but love you," I said as a single tear slipped down my cheek. "I know, baby, and I'm sorry; I'm so sorry," he said, breathing heavily with his hands in the air. "And you...all you ever did was take, take, take."

"Is this what you want? To kill me? I know you don't want to do this shit, Chan. I know you hate me right now, but even through all that, you still love me. Just put the gun down, baby. Put it down and I promise it'll be different, okay? I don't love her. I don't. I swear to God, I don't. I only love you and my kids, baby. You got my heart. No other broad can take that from you. You still got me, I swear."

The sounds of his pleads made my ears bleed. My head was spinning a million miles a minute. The air in the room was thin and my vision was getting blurrier by the second. Soon, all I heard was the sound of my heartbeat, increasing with every breath I took.

"You're right," I told him as I cocked the gun.

"Chan! Stop! Just think about what you're doing!" he yelled. There was no more thinking for me to do. There was no more talking, no more crying, no more anything. My mind was made up. "I do love you, Terrence. I love you to death."

POW, POW, POW

I told him as I pulled the trigger three times. One bullet for him, one for my broken heart, and one for the man I longed for him to be but he never would.

May 3, 2017

So you see, Your Honor, I would be lying if I sat here and told you that I didn't mean to kill him, or that I didn't *want* to kill him. He deserved it. He deserved every single bullet I lodged into his body that night. In love, just like in life, two people can look at the same thing and see something very different. As for me, I used to see forever, but he didn't. That night, I learned one of the toughest lessons I'd ever learned. Nothing lasts forever...not even love.

With that, I stepped off the stand and was escorted back to my seat with handcuffs wrapped around my wrists. The judge and jury wanted to hear my truth, so I gave it to them. So yeah, I did it. I killed him. Am I sorry about it? Hell no. Truth was, he cheated. Truth was, I still loved him, but I would be lying if I said I would ever forgive him. But hey, that's just the way love goes.

THE END

A DUSTY, SINCERE EVENING
Author Lette

As she sat in the café, she made the conscious decision that tonight; she was going to find someone to make her bitch for the night. Dusty thought, *this is it. This is the night I will throw out all of my inhibitions and just go for it. I sit around and play it so safe, but tonight, I feel like a little bit of danger.* After she sat there for about two minutes, frozen in the same spot as she was an hour before, she started to chuckle to herself. She knew that she was just kidding herself, but who was she fooling? She wanted too so badly, but on the other hand, not really. But it was an exciting thought for the moment.

Dusty was too much of a prude to do such a thing. Desiree "Dusty" Caldwell was a woman who wanted an exciting, more vibrant life, but the reality was that she was just a 32-year-old bank teller, who possessed a wild imagination without the wild heart to match.

"Dusty?"

Dusty was daydreaming while sitting at lunch with her best friend, Wanda, and did not hear her calling her name.

"Dusty, are you in there?" Wanda asked.

Dusty snapped back into reality, just in time to hear Wanda say, "This skank is in another world," as she laughed.

Dusty laughed as well, as she answered, "Fuck you, Wanda."

As the laughter continued, Wanda said, "You better not bail on me tonight, Dust. This is the big thirty-five for me and you know how you do. It is my birthday and I will not take you canceling on me with some lame-ass excuse, as you are known to do." Dusty could not debate with Wanda on this, because it was in fact, true.

A Dusty, Sincere Evening

She was a true homebody; an old maid as she was known to call herself every so often, but tonight she had no plans of letting her girl down. Wanda went on, "'Cause you know I need my wingman close by my side tonight to make sure that I behave myself."

Dusty knew her role. They kept each other in check, no matter the consequence. That is what made them such good friends. They looked out for one another. "I promise; I will not let you down, my friend."

"You better not," Wanda said as she grabbed her purse and her cell phone, and stood up to leave. She had some more things that she needed to do before her party tonight.

Dusty stood up, hugged Wanda and gave her a sisterly kiss on the cheek and said, "I got you, sis. Your wingman always got you."

CHAPTER 2

Dusty arrived at Club Blacker Berry just before 9 pm to celebrate her best friend, Wanda's birthday. She pulled up in her one big purchase in life besides her home, a custom-painted baby blue Jaguar with flecks of silver within the paint job. Dusty may be what she called herself, an old maid or a prude, but she was far from an old maid or prude within the looks department. When she stepped out of her Jaguar, she always gave the people what they wanted. Six feet of absolute gorgeousness, she wore a royal blue, two-piece skirt set, which clung to every curve of her voluptuous body. She was not a fan of the gym and actually went maybe seven to eight times a month, if that; her good eating habits helped her to keep her killer frame.

As she walked across the corridor and entered the club, all eyes were on her. Her long flowing auburn-colored hair fell across her shoulders and stopped midway down her back. Her fair-colored, smooth and flawless skin glistened in the night light, revealing a fresh dewy glow.

Her outfit, a mid-drift top that revealed her rock hard abs, a form fitting skirt that stopped just above her knees topped off with a pair of six-inch silver stilettos tied up her legs, caught the attention of every man and every women as she stepped into the club. She saw the birthday girl and headed towards her table at the front of the room. Dusty felt like a movie star. Maybe, just maybe she thought, her leaving the comfort of her home sanctuary this night would be worth it.

CHAPTER 3

Sincere Ra`Skins spotted her when she walked into the club, with an air of confidence in her stride. She was stunning. She was the star of the night. He knew every man in the club that night wanted her, including him, but after a keen observation of the situation going on around her table, he decided to sit back and let this one pass. She obviously was a woman who already had a slew of men at her beck and call, he imagined. Sincere, a 36-year-old garbage man from the South Side of Chicago was just in town for the weekend, tying up some loose ends before making his final venture out of Chicago.

He'd recently moved to Iowa City, IA from the Windy City, where he'd spent all of his life. Recently, he'd decided that he needed a change of pace; a step outside of the norm, so he had applied for a position as District Manager of the Department of Sanitation in Iowa City after seeing the posting on an online job site. After many months of going back and forth for interviews, he was blessed to be offered the position, in which he readily accepted. He immediately began to prepare for the move and had been going back and forth to Iowa, getting his relocation business intact.

This weekend was to be one of his last weekend visits in town before his final departure in about three more weeks. Sincere watched Dusty all night, as she turned down guy after guy who came over to ask her for a dance, buy her a drink, or just try to sit down with her for general conversation. Sincere himself was not much of a partier, but came to the party with one of his homeboys from work, as sort of an unofficial going away get-together.

Paulo, his co-worker and very good friend, invited him out to the birthday party of one of his home girl's from his neighborhood.

Sincere was a workaholic and not a night lifer so he rarely hit the club scene, but since Paulo wanted to do something to celebrate his new venture, he decided to come and hang out with him for the night. It was hard to get him away from anything that had to do with his work. If he could work seven days a week and get away with it, he would.

He was sneaking a glance at Dusty from across the room when Paulo said, "Man, take your ass on over there. You've been staring at her all damn night." Sincere looked at Paulo with a confused look on his face and said, "What? Fuck you talking about?"

Paulo nodded his head in the direction of Dusty's table. "Shorty, over there. Dude, you have been eyeballing her all night. Just go on over there and holler at her." Sincere knew that he had been sneaking glances at Dusty all night, but he did not think he was that obvious until Paulo recognized it.

He tried to play it off. "Dude, ain't nobody paying shorty no attention like that, bro."

Paulo looked at him and said, "Man, get the fuck out of here!" He laughed and went on, "Dog, you're so fuckin' full of it." He continued to laugh.

"Cere, go on over there dude, and make your move."

Sincere knew he was caught up, but still tried to play it off.

"Man, whatever. Ain't nobody sweating her like that, dog. Besides, she already has her own fan club going on. Every dude that has come her way, she has played them all off to the left."

Paulo burst out laughing. "Dog, you ain't shit. I thought you said that you were not paying her any attention." He laughed even harder. "Dude, take your ass on over there, man, and get your mack on." Sincere wanted to, but refused to give Paulo the satisfaction of being right. This was one that he was just gonna end up having to let go.

CHAPTER 4

Dusty was outside the club, pacing furiously by her car. How could she have been so careless and left the car lights on? She was disappointed in herself but what got her blood boiling the most was that even though she'd left her lights on, no one had the decency to come into the club and let the DJ know to announce that the lights were left on. Someone had to notice the baby blue Jaguar out in the parking lot, with the lights glaring.

She stood by her car on the phone with AAA, who was trying to get ahold of roadside service to come give her a jump. After she ended her the call, she opened up her trunk looking for the parka that she kept in her in her safe bag. The safe bag was a bag that she left in the trunk of her car at all times, furnished with materials needed in case of an emergency. The temperature had dropped drastically from the time she arrived at the club and this was most definitely a chilly emergency.

As she was putting on her parka, someone asked, "Is everything alright?" The voice from behind startled her. Dusty turned as Sincere was approaching her car. "Do you need any help?" *Damn, he fine*, she thought as she laid eyes on the 6'3", stocky-framed, dark-skinned specimen of a man. Sincere had come outside for a cigarette and to get away from the noise in the club for a while, when he saw Dusty pacing by her car, talking on the phone.

He did not approach her initially, not wanting to invade her privacy in case she was on the line with her boyfriend or husband. He figured that was why she was playing every dude in the club to the left. Then again, he imagined there was no way a lady of her caliber could possibly be single. He continued, "I saw that you were having some trouble with your car, so I came over to see if maybe I could assist you in some way?" Dusty couldn't help but stare at him. *Lord, was he fine.* She replied, "No. Like a dingbat, I left my lights on in the car. I turned them on manually earlier today during a safety inspection check, and evidently neglected to turn the setting back to automatic, where they would go off automatically.

So now, here I am with a dead cell in the battery." She felt a little foolish for being so careless; apparently too busy being a diva for the night that she did not even notice the warning when she stepped out of the car earlier that evening. "And as I stand here, I can honestly say that when I arrived, I remember hearing the warning buzzer that the lights were still on, but I was trying to hurry up and scurry into the club to avoid the hoopla. I obviously was not paying it any attention and now here I am, waiting on AAA. Who by the way, says that it may be up to two hours before they can even get to me. I could have been more than halfway home by now."

Sincere was thinking the entire time she was talking that he was glad that she did leave the lights on because she was stunning from afar, but up close, she was absolutely breathtaking. He said, "Well if all you need is a jump, I can help with that. No need to stay here for another hour or so just to have someone come and give your battery a jump." Dusty studied his mannerisms, his frame, his speech, his eyes and his lips as he spoke. He continued, "My car is just over on the other side of the building. I can head over and get it and have you on your way in no time."

Dusty was ready to go home and really did want her car started but this handsome gentleman had her intrigued, so she decided on a different route. "I don't know a lot about cars, but I do know that the battery is somewhere under the trunk of my car, and I'm not sure exactly how difficult it is to get to, so maybe we should just wait on AAA. Besides, I would not want you to get your outfit all dirty. That would tarnish that good look you have going on tonight," she flirted.

Sincere blushed and smiled at her compliment. He said, "No, it would not be a problem. I can't leave such a beautiful lady out here in distress. That would not be the gentlemanly thing to do." He admired her framework and was aroused by the sound of her sultry voice. Why was he trying to rush her off? He thought, *shut up, dummy!* He wanted to get to know her and he was clearly fucking it all up. Now Dusty was blushing. She replied, "We can just wait on AAA."

Sincere's eyebrows went up. "We?"

She smiled, "Yeah, if you don't mind. I really don't want to go back inside and I could use the company." Sincere did not mind. He didn't mind at all.

CHAPTER 5

"Oh my God, I can't believe that I am doing this," Dusty whispered.

Sincere picked her up and carried her to her bedroom. "Well, believe it," he replied. Sincere placed his lips on Dusty's as they made their way down the hall towards her bedroom. He continued kissing her lips and planting light kisses on her face. Placing Dusty on the bed, he began to remove her skirt, easing it slowly across her hips, down her body; teasing her while undressing her with his eyes. He wanted her so badly; his excitement took over him so much that he ripped her thong right off of her body.

"Sincere," Dusty whispered, breathing heavily. Sincere caressed her hot wet spot gingerly and then abruptly entered her with his hand, moving it in and out, building up the juices within her walls. He watched Dusty's every move as she cried out for joy and began making love to his hand, placing her hand on top of his, pushing it further inside her love dungeon with every in and out motion. It had been several months since she was touched in this way and Sincere was phenomenal with his sensually-geared hand coordination. He reached up with his free hand and caressed her C-cup breasts, as he dug deeper into her, rotating his hand, giving her immense pleasure with every stroke.

Sincere removed his hand from her inner sanctum, pulled her to the edge of the bed, got on the floor, down on his knees and placed light kisses all over the lips of her vagina, tonguing and teasing it, making her want more with every touch of his full lips. He drove her mad with anticipation. Dusty, not wanting to wait anymore to witness the full experience of what was Sincere, reached over to the nightstand as he sipped on her sexual juices, pulled out a condom and proceeded to hand it to him. Sincere looked at it, took it from her hand and threw it across the room.

Dusty shocked, spoke softly, "Why did you do that?" He crawled up the bed, braced himself over top of her body and stared into her eyes.

"Dusty, I want you." He licked his lips and placed a soft gentle kiss upon hers and said, "And I want all of you."

Dusty gazed into his eyes and saw that he was struck with a passion that even she was not going to be able to make him contain. Sincere kissed her neck passionately. He suckled her breast with such care, as if he was a newborn baby being nourished and feeding from her soul. He grabbed her hand and placed it on his massive member, instructing her to prepare it for insertion.

She abided by his direction, but pleaded, "Sincere, what are you doing?" Sincere gazed into her eyes and said nothing. He pushed his shaft into her slowly. Dusty cried out from the pleasure he was placing upon her loins. He bit his bottom lip, moaning at the feeling of her every muscle as they tightly constricted upon his member, savoring the feel of what he could only describe as absolute pure bliss.

Slowly, he invaded the space of her walls with his magnetic energy, giving her what she needed. She began to grind on his member, taking in everything that he had to give. And boy was he giving it to her. She caught every pitch he threw at her and pocketed every dime he placed in her love bank. Sincere, placing his hands and firmly gripping her bottom, lifted Dusty's pelvis up off of the bed, and began sliding in and out of her, causing her to take every inch of him into her world. Sincere grunted with every pass, every stroke, every movement and every thrust he strongly placed upon Dusty's wet loins.

Dusty met his every move with such force as their bodies slapped together, filling the room with the sounds of a beautiful slow jam written just for them.

She cursed, groaned, and moaned between thrusts until her pace quickened, as her body prepared her for a climatic release. Sincere quickened his pace to meet her every move, needing to see her face and look into her eyes. He placed his weight on her body, causing her to lie back on the bed and whispered, while staring into her eyes.

"Let me see it, baby. Give it to me. Cum and drown me with that shit." Dusty grabbed his bottom, pulling him deeper inside of her with each pounding until her body began to shiver and shake, erupting and giving him exactly what he wanted. Sincere did not give her a chance to catch her breath. He began to move in and out of her slowly. Breathing heavily, she spoke softly, 'Sincere, you have got to stop.

We can't do this." She moaned in the middle of her statement. "Sincere, I-I don't...Ooooooo, shiiiit." Sincere watched her facial expressions. She tried to continue, "Pleeeease...Sinceeeeere, we can't dooooooo...aaaaaah, fuuuuck." Sincere listened to and loved the sounds of her hot wet spot as he grinded into her, covering him with all of her sexual juices. Dusty, with difficulty, was finally able to squeal out, "Sincere, waaaaait... I don't take any preg...pregnancy protect......tection."

He reached down and kissed her soft full lips. Sincere made love to her mouth, playing a game of tag with her tongue; biting and suckling her bottom lip until her lips were swollen and red, while continuing to move in and out of her with precise precision. He watched this beauty releasing her body and part of her soul to him and he knew. He knew and there was no doubt in his mind; he had fallen in love in one night. Had fallen in love at first sight and had fallen hard for who he knew was his heart's downfall. That out of all of his conquests over the years, this woman was the only woman who ever made him feel alive.

He did not know everything about her but he knew that he loved her and that their chance meeting was absolute fate. He knew that AAA taking two and a half hours was enough time to know that he had found the love of his life, the woman who would be his wife. Even he knew that it sounded crazy, but no one could make him feel anything any different. Not even Dusty. His pace once again quickened as his body could no longer hold back his excitement.

Knowing what he knew, Sincere came up for air long enough to whisper softly, "Good, because you're mine." He released, erupting within her walls, with the hope and expectation of making this woman his everything, including the mother of his children. He released into her all of his hopes, dreams, goals and even part of his soul. He collapsed upon her chest, panting and gasping for air. They lay in silence, in the quiet of the night, with nothing but the smell of their evening lingering in the room all around them. He looked up at her, looking so beautiful and said, "Dusty?"

She looked into his eyes as a single tear ran down her cheek, "Yes?"

He reached up and wiped the tear from her face. "I love you." Dusty closed her eyes and the tears started to flow.

Dusty thought back to earlier in the day at the café when she was joking with herself about throwing out all of her inhibitions, just taking a chance for once in her life. *How could this be happening?* she thought. Sincere laid his head upon her chest, listening to her heartbeat, studying the rhythm, wanting and needing so desperately for it to match his. Dusty had never done anything like this before, but she wanted him. All of him. From the moment that she saw him. Dusty placed her hand on his face, stroked his cheek and replied, "I love you too."

ABUSED BY LOVE
Author Nisha Lanae

Night had fallen and the Steinberg household had wound down. Miranda was headed back to her room after tucking her daughters in for the night. As she neared her room, she heard the creak of the front door downstairs in the foyer. Miranda glanced over at the grandfather clock that hung in the bedroom she shared with her husband; it was a little after ten o'clock, which was early for her husband to be home on a Friday night.

Miranda nestled under the covers grabbing the *Essence Magazine* from the nightstand and finished reading the article she had started earlier. Miranda went to turn the page and noticed Wyatt. Miranda's heart swelled, glancing at the sexy smirk on his face as he leaned on their bedroom door with his hands tucked in his pants pocket. The olive green, three-piece tailored suit fit his 5'11" muscular frame just right. His icy blue eyes piercing right through her instantly caused the spot in between her legs to get moist. His working many late nights had caused them to be on different schedules all month, leaving her lonely and her body yearning for his touch.

"Hey there, handsome," she smiled, pushing a loose strand of hair behind her ear. "You're home early," Miranda spoke bashfully. The smell of whiskey, cigars and his Gucci cologne danced around Miranda's nostrils, causing her nipples to harden through the thin fabric of the nightgown she had on as he neared her. His eyes glued to her.

The haughty look that quickly appeared in his eyes puzzled her for a moment, until he reached the bed and his lips spread into a wide smile. Using one hand, he gently stroked the nape of her neck.

Miranda closed her eyes, loving the feel of his tender touch. Suddenly, Miranda's eyes bulged as she felt him grip the nape of her neck.

"Miranda, my beautiful black queen. Who have you been entertaining in my house when I am not home?" Wyatt tilted her head back by the nape of her neck forcing her to look him in the eye. "Wyatt, what are you talking about?" Miranda questioned, puzzled by his accusations.

"Miranda honey, don't lie to me. Did you have someone in my house?"

"You sound crazy. The girls and I are the only people who have been here. You must have had way too much to drink tonight. You are in here talking crazy," Miranda replied, trying to wiggle out of his grip.

"Don't fuckin' sass me. Now, who did you have in my house? I am only going to ask you one last time," Wyatt demanded, wrapping his hands around Miranda's neck.

"Please," Miranda pleaded. She tried to get his hands from around her neck. But, the more she tried to pry his hands from her neck, the more he applied pressure. His eyes were full of rage which scared Miranda; she never saw the haughty look in his eyes before tonight. She didn't know what made him act so crazed.

"Miranda, don't play with me. Now someone saw a man come in this house. What man are you sneaking in my house? Who is he? Is he a nigger like you, bitch? I should have listened when they told me not to marry your black ass," Wyatt spat nastily, gripping her neck tighter.

"No..." Miranda struggled to let out.

Releasing his grip on her neck, Wyatt stood and watched as Miranda instantly went into a coughing fit, struggling to breathe. It took several moments for Miranda to regain her normal breathing pattern before she was able to speak.

"What in the hell is your problem, Wyatt? You could have killed me," Miranda wailed.

"Shut the hell up," Wyatt yelled, pushing Miranda back on the bed. "I told you to stop lying to me and playing with my emotions. I told you to never cheat on me. You promised you wouldn't." His eyes softened, displaying an ounce of hurt. "I love you. Why do you insist on making me crazy? Who is the man you are sleeping with? Do I know him? What is his name?" he questioned.

"There is no other man. The only man I am sleeping with is you. My husband." Tears fell from Miranda's eyes, feeling hurt that he would even think she would give herself to someone else. She hadn't laid eyes on another man since they had been together.

Seeing her cry only angered Wyatt further. "You want to fuck around? Huh?" Wyatt questioned unfastening his belt and letting his pants fall to his ankles. His semi-erect penis peeked through his boxer briefs. "Since you like being a fucking whore, I'm going to treat you like one." Pushing Miranda back on the bed, he pushed her nightgown up revealing her freshly waxed vagina. A wicked grin formed on his face.

"Honey?" Miranda paused. "Wh-what are you doing?" Miranda asked, panic riddled in her voice. The look in his eyes was something she had never seen and it was scaring the hell out of her. He was acting like someone she didn't know.

POW!

Wyatt's hand landed across her face. "I told you to never question me. You want to be a whore and lie to me? I am going to treat you like a whore. You black bitch." Pushing her legs apart, he pulled out his fully hardened penis, forcefully penetrating her.

"Wyatt, stop! You are acting crazy," Miranda cried, trying to push him off of her. But it was to no avail, he was much too powerful. Miranda gave up and laid there thinking, how things had gotten so bad for Wyatt and her. Was her husband actually on top of her raping her? Was it rape? Could a husband rape his wife? The questions swarmed around Miranda's head as she listened to Wyatt moan and grunt on top of her.

Wyatt had hit her in the past a few times, but never had he forced himself on her. He had never been given a reason to. Any time he wanted it, Miranda was there on his beck and call to serve him like a king, in any way he requested.

"Shit," Wyatt shrieked. With one hand, he gripped Miranda by her neck as he pulled his penis out of her, releasing his hot semen on her stomach. "Ooooohhhhh shit. That is like a little slice of heaven between your legs," he boasted. "Let me find out you giving my sweet black pussy to some other man. Miranda, darling," he paused. "I will kill you with my bare hands and any man you attempt to share your body with besides me." Wyatt threatened in her ear as his tongue circled her earlobe.

"Of course not," Miranda shook her head in bewilderment.

"Better not. If you know what's best for you." Wyatt chuckled, making his way towards the master bathroom.

Miranda laid there for a moment, still trying to process what had just happened between Wyatt and her. Finally gathering her bearings, Miranda made her way into their shared master bathroom. Miranda didn't even look in his direction as she slipped the nightgown over her head and stepped into the hot water to wash away his sins. Her body reeked of him. Miranda washed and washed, trying to scrub away the layer of tainted skin. She was still in shock that Wyatt had done something so erratic.

"Trying to wash that other man away from you?" Wyatt questioned.

Miranda's eyes flew to the door where Wyatt was standing in his boxers, drinking a cold beer. She hadn't even realized how long she had been in the shower. Instead of saying something wrong and pissing him off any further, Miranda just turned off the water and grabbed her towel to dry off. Miranda slid into a t-shirt and prepared to get back in bed, intending to go to sleep and try to mentally escape what had just happened to her. She so desperately wanted to crawl in a corner and decay away. Just as she neared the custom king-size bed, she was stopped abruptly. "Where do you think you are going?" Wyatt questioned.

"To bed," Miranda replied dryly, trying not to look him in his eyes.

"You will not be sleeping in here, since you cannot tell the truth. You do not deserve to sleep next to me in the bed I purchased for me and my wholesome wife, not the whore that she is turning into." Wyatt frowned.

"I am not a whore," Miranda replied low. "I am still the same woman you married. It's you who changed." Miranda finally gained the courage to look Wyatt in his bright eyes, silently begging for her lovely husband to return. A lone tear fell on her honey cocoa cheek, which infuriated Wyatt.

"Don't start all that crying, Miranda. You weren't crying when you had another man in my damn house. No, you were too busy being a whore and giving another man what belongs to me. You belong to me," he screamed, slamming his hand on the nightstand on his side of the bed. "You will not sleep next to me until you realize that you belong to me and only me."

"Keep it down. You are going to wake the girls." Miranda spoke, her eyes going to their bedroom door, praying he hadn't awakened their daughters."Maybe I should go in there and tell them how much their mother is a whore."

"Wyatt, this is between you and I. Don't bring the girls into this," Miranda pleaded.

"Why are you doing this to us, honey? Making me act all crazy?" His voice softened again as if he was on the verge of crying.

His actions puzzled Miranda. It was like he was torn between two people. It scared Miranda. "Wyatt, I think you should get some help. I haven't done anything. I promise."

"Just get out. I am tired of looking at you," Wyatt spat.

Miranda glanced back at Wyatt before she walked out the room. Miranda peeked in on the girls before settling in the guest room.

The next morning

Miranda sat at the breakfast nook at her mother-in-law's house, staring at the wall. The events of the previous night kept replaying in her mind. She vowed years ago, after her mother was killed by the hands of her lover; she would never let a man put his hands on her. She had two little girls looking up to her and staying in this dysfunctional relationship was something she couldn't see herself doing after what Wyatt had done. But, she was afraid he wouldn't let her just leave him.

He had crossed the line and she wasn't sure what else he would do. Was he capable of murder? He was someone different. His eyes and the way he looked at her were so off. She couldn't shake the haughty look in his eyes. Her heart was broken and her mind was in a million places.

"Miranda, you've been here for almost two hours and haven't said much. What's on your mind?" Darlene questioned.

"I'm just not feeling well." Miranda glanced at her mother-in-law, offering her a soft smile.

"What's wrong with you?" Miranda's body tensed. She didn't know where he had come from. She hadn't heard his car or the front door open. His presence slightly frightened her. "Mother," Wyatt spoke, his eyes focusing on Miranda. "Are you sick? You look fine to me."

"Son, how is everything going down there at the office? I heard from Katie that Brad was caught in another scandal. This time with an underage girl. What a shame. His mother should be ashamed of the little bitch she raised. Had she been less concerned about being on her knees to every man that looked her damn way, she would have raised a better one. You should seriously consider separating the family business from the business you share with him."

"Mother, don't be so hard on him. Brad is a good guy. He is just going through a tough time right now. It doesn't help his wife is a whore and has screwed half of his colleagues. Once he gets rid of her, he will be back to his old self."

"Oh save that bullshit. Brad has been trouble since you guys were kids. Don't blame that woman. Blame his mother. I personally like Sasha."

"Okay, Mother," Wyatt replied, not wanting to go back and forth with his mother. "Darling, I don't want you hanging around Sasha anymore either," Wyatt informed, focusing his attention back on Miranda.

"Why?" Miranda questioned. Sasha was his business partner, Brad's, wife. She was the only friend he had allowed Miranda to maintain a friendship with.

"Darling, didn't I tell you to never question me?" Wyatt came closer to Miranda, causing her to slightly jump.

"Like I said, stay away from Sasha. She is a whore. I don't need her further tainting you. I will see you later. Make sure you get the girls in before it get late," he spoke, planting a soft kiss on her cheek. "Remember what I told you last night." He winked.

"Okay," Miranda replied dryly.

"See you later, Mother."

"Later, Wyatt," Darlene replied. She waited until she heard Wyatt's car pull out the driveway. "So are you going to tell me what is really going on?"

"I am not sure what you mean."

"Don't bullshit me. You practically jumped out of your skin when your husband came close to you. Has Wyatt ever put his hands on you?"Darlene pried.

"No," Miranda lied. She knew if Wyatt found out she was telling their business, things would only escalated worse in their household. She wasn't prepared for that.

"And I guess I am seeing things. A woman's natural instinct isn't to jump when her husband nears her. Unless he is abusing her..."

"Darlene, please just leave it alone. I don't want to set him off any more than he is already."

"Set him off?"Darlene asked, baffled.

"Yeah." Miranda nodded. "It's like; he hasn't been himself these last few weeks. He has been coming home drunk, speaking more vague to me and last night he accused me of having another man in our house.

He thinks I am cheating." Miranda lost it and broke down crying. "I would never cheat on him."

"Stop that crying. Everything is going to be okay. He's just going through a lot with the business and his business partner isn't worth a damn. Make no mistake, that doesn't give him the right to put his hands on you. You can say he hasn't. But, I have been on this earth far longer then you and have been around the block a few times. I have had my share of making excuses for the man I loved. You are beautiful. Make no excuse for a man disrespecting you. If he does it once, trust; he will do it again, no matter how many times he says he won't do it again. Remember, you have daughters watching."

"Do you mind watching the girls for an hour? I just need to take a drive and clear my head. I don't want them to see me like this,"Miranda asked. At that moment being around Darlene, she felt translucent, like a thin sheet of paper.

"Go ahead."

Miranda made a beeline to the door. She needed to talk to someone who was going to give her the truth.As soon as Miranda pulled out of Darlene's driveway, she headed to look for Sasha. She needed advice and Sasha always had some.

Miranda's heels clicked against the marble floor as she made swift strides through Sasha's upscale spa. Without knocking, she pushed the office door open and there was Sasha, bent over the desk with her skirt hiked up around her waist, as a young beau sucked on her clitoris like his life depended on it. The sight slightly aroused Miranda.

"Ahem," Miranda cleared her throat, making her presence known.

Sasha tilted her head to the side to see who was interrupting her. "Awww shit, Miranda. I'm busy, come back," Sasha moaned.

"I can't. This is the only time I have."

"Fuck," Sasha grunted. "Ashton, baby, give me a few moments to speak with my friend."

"Okay." The man, who slightly resembled Vin Diesel, grabbed his shirt from the floor. "Your new flavor of the week?" Miranda teased. "I heard the latest with Brad. I see it is not affecting you much."

"I don't care what the man I am married to does. Love has long vanished. I'm here out of convenience. But, you look like you just lost your best friend. "What is going on?" Sasha questioned.

"It's Wyatt. I don't know what is going on with him. He hasn't been acting like himself lately. Last night, he accused me of cheating on him and called me all sorts of whores and black bitches."

"He has his damn nerve," Sasha frowned. "Didn't his punk ass pursue you?"

"Yeah, but he has changed. He isn't that same guy. Last night, he had a look in his eye that I've never seen before. Today, as his mother is going in on Brad, he tells me he doesn't want me hanging around you because you're a whore," Miranda blurted.

"And he is a coke head," Sasha spat.

"What? Wyatt is a lot of things, but he wouldn't use drugs. I know that for a fact," Miranda spoke, thinking, *it would explain his recent actions if he was on drugs*. But, he hated drugs, which is why he cut all communication with his younger brother and his father, before his untimely death.

No, Wyatt couldn't be on drugs.

"Forget I even said that. Like I told you before, Miranda, you have to get a backbone and stop letting that husband of yours control you. Have you tired talking to him and seeing what is going on with him?"

Miranda crooked her neck, looking at Sasha like she was crazy. "We are speaking about Wyatt. There is not talking to that man."

"So what is your next step? You cannot keep letting him control your life."

"I am scared. I don't have anything. If I leave him, I will be leaving with nothing. I signed a pre-nuptial agreement. But, I don't want to raise my daughters with them seeing me be hit on and controlled. Then they will think it's okay to be done to them. I watched my mother go through it. I don't want my daughters to have the same fears I had growing up. But, I know he isn't going to just allow me to leave him." Miranda paused and looked at Sasha before she began to speak again. "Has Brad ever forced himself on you?"

"What do you mean, 'force?' Like I told him I wasn't in the mood and he kept going?"

"Something like that. Do you think a husband can rape his own wife?"

"Rape is rape. If you say no and they keep going, that is rape. I don't care if it is your husband." Sasha paused and replayed Miranda's question over in her head. "Miranda, did Wyatt rape you?" Sasha questioned, her eyes prying into Miranda. Miranda put her head down in shame. She couldn't bear to look Sasha in the eye. "Last night... after he went into a fit of rage and accused me of having another man in the house. He forced himself on me and told me since I was acting like a whore; he would treat me like one."Miranda tried to hold back the tears, but couldn't.

"What?" Sasha questioned, rushing over to Miranda nearly in tears. "Look at me. You do not deserve this. I am so sorry this happened to you. I have never told a woman what she should do in her relationship. But, Miranda, you need to leave him, even if it is for a short while so he can get his shit in order. You can't stay there. What will be next? Is he hitting you?"

Miranda just nodded her head up and down, as a sea of tears cascaded down her cheeks.

"Fucking coward," Sasha mumbled.

"Sasha, I am so baffled. I don't know what went wrong in our marriage for him to think I would step out of our marriage. Since I met him, I have only had eyes for him."

"He is a man. Sometimes they do and say dumb shit to cover up what they really are doing."

"You think it's another woman? Could he be the one cheating?"

"Do you think he is cheating?" Sasha questioned, trying to make sure her words were chosen wisely.

"I don't know. All I know is I love my husband. But, I don't know who he has become and I am scared. Scared if I stay, one day he may come home in a fit of rage and kill me. Scared if I leave, I won't have shit. My kids are accustomed to a certain lifestyle. I can't give them that without him, and I don't want my kids to be raised without their father."

"You sound crazy. Do you know how many single mothers are out there doing it on their own without the help of a man, Miranda? You are beautiful and educated. I promise you will be good." Before meeting and marrying Wyatt Steinberg, the CEO of Steinberg Construction and COO of Reality Group Corporation, Miranda had just received her master's degree in human resources and was brought on to the company to be in charge of their labor department. Falling head over heels for the tall and handsome, blue-eyed, red-haired CEO, the wide smiled socialite slowly started to change and became more of the woman Wyatt wanted.

"I haven't worked in over eight years. Who will hire me? Wyatt would make sure I never worked anywhere."

"Who said you would need to work? Do you know why I am still with Brad?"

"No."

"Because just like you; I was young and head over heels for that man. Since he already had money and I was in love with him, I signed the pre-nuptial agreement that states I get basically nothing. Not even the damn house. I been with that damn man for twelve years and put up with a lot of shit. I'll be damned if I leave empty-handed."

"How are you going to do that?"

"And I thought black women were smarter than us white bitches?" Sasha laughed. "Didn't you walk in here and tell me about some damn scandal with that man I am married to?"

"Yeah?"

Sasha smirked. "My point."

Miranda stared back at Sasha, perplexed on what she was trying to imply. "Are you truly ready to leave Wyatt?"

Miranda sat and pondered the question. She was still confused. A part of her wanted to leave him, and another part still loved him and wanted their marriage to work.

"You are not sure. I get it and trust me, I understand. So I am going to look into some things that I feel will work best for you. Once I have them done, I will let you make the choice. As of right now, I want you to go home and be the good little wife. Make his favorite dinner and when he gets home, fuck him like you are his personal porn star. What I am about to say next may confuse you. But, as much as you can, I need you to push what happened last night to the back of your mind. Far enough where you still remember it happened. And every time you think about staying with him, remember it. You got it?"

Miranda repeated what Sasha told her over in her head, before she nodded her head in agreement.

"Good, now get home and start working on dinner. I will let you know what I have planned next and see if you are with it."

"Okay." Miranda got up and headed for the door.

"Miranda?" Sasha called out.

Miranda turned and faced Sasha. "You are going to be alright. I promise."

"Thank you." Miranda smiled.

"Oh and the underage girl my husband was caught with is actually an underage boy with a sex change. He transitioned into a girl," Sasha laughed.

Miranda's eyes bulged as her hand flew to her mouth in shock. She knew right then and there Sasha had everything to do with Brad's downward spiral. She couldn't help but laugh as she made her way out the spa. Miranda made it back to Darlene's, just as the sun was going down. "Maddie, Olivia," Miranda called out for her daughters as she entered her mother-in-law's house with a wide grin on her face.

"I guess that drive did you some justice. That smile looks great on you."

"Thanks for watching the girls for me."

"You are more than welcome."

"Mommy," the girls giggled as they ran into the foyer to greet their mother. "Grandma let us plant our own flowers in the garden today."

"Oh really? Well, what kind of flowers did you plant?"

"They were..." Olivia paused, trying to remember what her grandmother had told her. "Umm...Grandma, what did you call them again?"

"Tuli..." Maddie spoke, trying to remember

"Tulips," Darlene advised.

"They were tulips," the girls chimed with bright smiles.

"That's nice. Once they grow, you can bring some home for Mommy."

"Yeah, Mommy, can we have a garden at our house?"

"Sure baby, maybe Grandma can come and help get it started," Miranda spoke, eyeing Darlene and begging her with her eyes. Miranda didn't know anything about gardening.

"Anything for my pretty girls. Miranda, he is my son. But, I am a woman first. Abuse is never over. Keep smiling; you are going to be alright. " Darlene smiled. "Now get home safe."

"Okay," Miranda replied. Hearing those simple words twice in one hour made her smile. Maybe they saw a strength in her she had forgotten. "Who wants ice cream?" Miranda questioned the girls as they headed out the door.

"Me!" the girls yelled as they walked out the door and rushed to their mother's car.

A few weeks later

Miranda's heart pumped a mile a minute as she pulled into the parking lot of U.S. Bank. True to her word, Sasha had come up with a perfect plan to move money from Wyatt and Brad's business account that she had gained access to. She created an offshore account in a non-profit organization. She then had an identification created in another name for Miranda to withdraw the money. Miranda then would open a safe deposit box in another name to hide the money, until she felt she had enough money stashed.

Miranda pulled into a parking space, applied a fresh coat of lipstick and checked herself in the mirror before stepping out the car. She straightened out the Aspen pencil skirt she wore, accompanied by the three-quarter length blazer. She looked every part of a wealthy woman. Diamond stud earrings adored her ears, her large diamond studded wedding ring shined bright on her finger, and a single diamond drop necklace. Grabbing her handbag, Miranda made her way inside the bank, saying a silent prayer that everything worked out perfect for her.

"Welcome to U.S. Bank. Is there anything I can assist you with today?"

"Yes, I was looking to open a safe deposit box."

"Sure, I will get a personal banker for you."

"Thanks."

The young girl disappeared behind a security door. Miranda scanned the lobby, which had only a few customers, mostly older people. Just as Miranda turned back around, the young girl was headed back her way with a tall, young black man in tow. "Hello, I am Justin Smalls; I will be your personal banker today. Yaseina said you were interested in opening a safe deposit box?"

"Yes, I have some personal items I need to put away."

"Well, I will be happy to assist you with that. Miss?"

"It's Mrs. Dionna Sanders."

"Right this way, Mrs. Sanders."

Miranda's heart pumped as she handed Justin the identification and paperwork Sasha had provided her. She watched him closely as he stepped a few feet over to make copies of everything. What felt like countless hours, was merely only a few minutes.

"We are all done. I will show you to your box." Justin smiled.

"Wow, that was fast."

"You had everything ready, which made it a smooth process. This is you. Here is your box information. I will leave you alone. Just exit the left door and security will be there waiting to walk you out. Thanks you for your business. I have attached my card. Don't hesitate to give me a call if you need anything," Justin smiled.

"Thanks," Miranda smiled. She waited until she heard the click of the door before she pulled the envelope out of her bag, safely placing it inside the space that would hold the future for her and her daughters. Once everything was inside the safe, Miranda exited the bank with a sense of relief overcoming her. Miranda made it to her car and a big smile spread across her face. She had safely moved a quarter of a million dollars for her future. This was a new high. Do you think Miranda will leave Wyatt? Stay tuned for the full story; it only gets juicer and will leave you on the edge of your seat.

THE DEVIL
IN RED LIPSTICK
Author Sha Jones

"Baby, please call me back as soon as you power your phone back on! I'm worried about you!" Eva cried as she held the phone up to her ear. It had been 10 hours since Eva heard from her husband Glen, and his unexplained absence was making her sick to her stomach. God, please let him be alright, Eva thought as she paced back and forth in the middle of her living room.

Eva was in such a panic with the thought that something could be seriously wrong with the man that she was deeply in love with, tears poured out of her eyes like a bucket of water. She had no clue where he was and knew that it was strange that her husband hadn't made it to the house already. He usually came straight home from work, but tonight he was nowhere in sight. As she stood there crying her eyes out, trying to figure out what might've happened to Glen, there was a loud knock at the door causing her to gasp for air. Eva was so alarmed and excited at the same time, her legs felt like they were going numb. God, please let this be him!

Eva darted for the door so fast she almost ran head first into the wall. She was shaking uncontrollably and just a total wreck. Before opening the door, she took a deep breath and prayed that it was Glen at the door. She imagined him standing there explaining to her how his car broke down and his phone went dead, so he had to wait until he was able to get a tow truck to scoop him from the side of the road. Eva took another deep breath, and opened the door, but was greeted by her twin sister, Evelyn, who was standing there with a concerned look on her face.

Eva and Evelyn were identical twins, and they looked so much alike that not even their close friends and family could sometimes tell them apart. They both shared the same beautiful brown skin complexion with a nice grade of hair.

Although they shared the same face, there were a few differences between them. Eva had expensive taste in cars, clothes, and designer bags. She loved to make herself up like a Barbie doll and never missed a hair or nail appointment.

Evelyn, on the other hand, preferred to wear her hair in a bun, didn't wear makeup, unless it was for a special occasion. Just like her sister, she was also married. Her husband, Stevie, was a very successful defense attorney, but she didn't let her husband's money and success change who she was.

"Oh my God, Eva, I got here as soon as I could!" Evelyn said as she grabbed her sister and held her in her arms. With the sisters being twins, Evelyn could literally feel her sister's pain to the point where she too was in tears and feeling deeply distraught.

"Don't worry, sis...We're going to find him, okay?" Evelyn cried as she walked in the house with her sister.

"I don't know what to do! I've been to his office, but he wasn't there. His car wasn't in the parking garage. I called his mother and his sister, and they haven't heard anything from him. This isn't like Glen," Eva said as she wiped the snot that was rolling from her nose with the back of her hand. She was so weakened by her husband's disappearance, her knees buckled just from talking about it. All of these negative thoughts then began running through her mind like bad traffic.

"Maybe he hung out with one of his co-workers or something," Evelyn sighed as she ran her fingers through her hair. Eva stared off into space with a blank look on her face.

"No, he would call me, Evelyn. He wouldn't just leave without telling me his plans."

Eva and Glen were very close and told each other everything. She loved her man with every fiber in her body, and he felt the same way about her. They had sex damn near every night, so as far as Eva was concerned, there was no reason for him to not want to come home to her or not communicate about his plans.

With tears still running down her cheeks, Eva looked at her sister with glossy eyes and asked, "What if he's not alive?"

Asking the heart twisting question out loud made Eva's chest burn, and the reality of what was going on was almost unbearable.

"God please," Eva begged as she dropped to her knees.

Evelyn suddenly dropped to her knees and wrapped her arms around her twin. She didn't know what to say or do to make things better or to persuade her sister that her husband was okay because she too felt like something was up. It wasn't like her brother-in-law to just leave without explanation, and it damn sure wasn't like him to let his phone go dead because from what she knew, Glen had a house charger as well as one for his car.

"Just pray, Eva," Evelyn cried out.

Eva was so hurt, she couldn't even find the strength to pray. "This isn't like him," she mumbled. Eva knew that if her husband didn't walk in the house by the morning, there was a possibility that he wasn't alive.

Two hours after Evelyn left, Eva found herself drifting in and out of consciousness. Every few minutes she called her husband's phone, but it continued to go to voicemail. She was so sleepy and exhausted from crying, that she could barely even stay up. Fear mixed in with fatigue was a combination that she couldn't handle and before she knew it, she was out like a light switch on the couch. While Eva slept, she saw images of Glen's car being split in half with his body hanging out of it. Blood was all over his face, and he was no longer alive.

She saw police trucks zooming up and down the streets as she stood on the sidelines watching in horror as her husband's crumpled body was being pulled out of his Mercedes. Just seeing the man that she spent seven years of her life with being placed into a black body back felt too real and painful. A part of Eva didn't want to be alive if she couldn't have her man with her.

Eva suddenly found herself breaking down and screaming, and when she finally woke up and opened her eyes, she was still screaming. Her dark living room was now filled with light, making it obvious that it was a new day.

Eva's heart was beating so fast she thought it was about to fall out of her chest. She took a deep breath, sat up on the couch, and wiped the sweat from her hairline. She then stared down at her phone that was clutched in her hand, and when she saw that she didn't have a text from Glen, she felt sick all over again.

"Oh, my God," she moaned as she tapped his name on her screen and put the phone to her ear. When it went straight to voicemail again, she was stunned. When she looked at the time and noticed that it was almost eight o'clock in the morning, she broke down. She was crying just as hard as she was last night because it was only confirmation that something was terribly wrong.

Even if her husband was out doing something he didn't have any business doing, he would never ignore her or not come home to eat and shower. Glen was a very well put together man, so skipping a shower wasn't something he would do. Not only that, Eva watched him leave for work yesterday morning, and all he had in his hand was his briefcase, an indication that he wasn't going out of town.

Eva sat on the couch replaying the last time she saw her husband and the sweet love that they made. Him saying, "I love you," floated through her head and only made things worse. She wasn't sure of what was going on, but she was praying like hell that this wouldn't be the last time that she would hear those sweet words roll from her husband's lips. 2

That afternoon, Eva paced back and forth in her living room once again, calling her husband's phone, but all it did was go to voicemail. She was so frustrated; she wanted to smash her phone into pieces.

"Fuck!" she screamed at the top of her lungs. Eva was annoyed for reasons, other than Glen being missing. She was irritated with the cops for not taking her husband's disappearance seriously and felt like they didn't give a damn about his well-being.

Their explanation to her was that he was a grown man, and he needed to be missing for at least 24 hours for her to even file a report, but Eva felt like within those hours, he would be dead. Eva spent most of the day on the phone with Glen's sister, Patrice, and her sister, trying to piece everything together. They each drove around trying to see if they could spot his vehicle, but Houston was so huge that trying to locate him was like looking for a needle in a haystack.

"Where the hell could he be?" Eva nervously asked. In a way, she felt silly as hell for not even knowing where her own husband was, what he was doing, or if he was even safe. It made her feel like she wasn't keeping her home in order.

"I don't know, but this isn't like my brother," Patrice sighed.

Patrice was usually calm and reserved when it came to certain situations, but she couldn't help but express her concern, especially by Glen being her big brother, and her only sibling. Their father passed away from prostate cancer, and their mother was pretty much the only family that they had, so the thought of her losing her brother was stressing her the hell out. Now that Patrice was concerned, it made Eva even more nervous and made her want to give up hope.

She was crying so bad her head felt like it was about to burst. While she was on the phone with her sister-in -aw, Eva's phone beeped, causing her heart to stop. Maybe this is him! she thought as she reached for her chest. Any little sound alarmed Eva because she just knew that it would be Glen walking through the door, but each time, she was disappointed. When she looked at the phone and saw her sister calling, she sighed and told Patrice that she would call her back.

Eva quickly clicked over and answered in a dry tone. "Hello."

"Hey sis, have you heard anything?" Evelyn asked nervously.

Eva shook her head and just sighed. She was feeling so weak she didn't even have the energy to talk anymore.

Evelyn could immediately sense her sister's emotions, and in a weird way knew exactly how she was feeling, so she decided that she could no longer sit back and watch her suffer.

"I'm coming to get you, Eva. You need to get the hell out of that house. Being there without knowing where Glen is, is too much for you right now."

Before Eva could say anything, Evelyn hung up the phone in her face. Eva nervously ran her fingers through her hair, dragged her legs over to the couch in defeat, and plopped down on it. She stared down at her phone and watched as her tears hit the screen. Although she wanted to give up, she wasn't ready to because she knew that if something went horribly wrong with her, she was absolutely sure that Glen would've done everything that he could to find her.

Eva took a deep breath as if she was about to be submerged into the deep blue ocean and dialed her husband's number again. "Please answer, baby," she mumbled as she carefully placed the phone to her ear.

"You have reached the voicemail of..." Eva hung up the phone, dropped it on the floor, and sobbed. Her body literally felt like it was deteriorating. Her mind couldn't take it anymore, and she was well beyond her breaking point. She was mentally and emotionally drained.

She was so tired of crying, she was surprised that she was even able to still produce tears. The fact that Glen had now been missing for 22 hours was more terrifying than anything that Eva had ever experienced in her life. Later that night, Eva stayed at her sister's house. She was finally able to file a police report, and it only made things worse because reality was finally settling in. While at the house, they turned on the TV and waited for the news to come on.

"I think he's dead," Eva said as she sat on the couch next to her sister biting her nails and shaking her legs.

"No, don't think like that!" Evelyn replied. She wasn't ready to accept that her brother-in-law might be dead, so she held on to a strong hope that it was something else. She shook her head at the thought and finally turned to her sister.

"Do you think that maybe he could be out with another woman?" Evelyn didn't want that to be the case, but if he was out creeping with another woman, at least he would be alive and well. Eva wiped the tears from her eyes, sighed and said, "I don't think he would do that, and even if he did go with another woman, he wouldn't just power his phone off, leaving me to wonder all day and night. He would've came home already, Eve."

"Yeah, that's true," Evelyn sighed.

"Well, I don't know, sis. Let's just try to remain positive."

"I don't think that I can even do that right now. I've tried to be optimistic, but with the way things are looking, I need to be realistic."

While Evelyn sat on the couch holding Eva in her arms, Stevie walked through the front door with a concerned look on his face. He adjusted his black tie that matched his suit and scratched his bushy beard. He knew what was going on with his sister-in-law, and his heart went out to her. Not only was he feeling awful for her, he too was feeling a great deal of sadness for himself because he and Glen were close. They both worked together as attorneys from time to time, so to now know that his friend and colleague was missing, was painful.

"Y'all heard anything?" he asked.

Evelyn stared up at her man with a defeated look on her face and slowly shook her head. Stevie sat his briefcase down by the door and ran his hands over his face in frustration.

"What the cops say?" he asked.

"Nothing really. We filed the report, and that was it. All we can do it just wait," Evelyn replied. Stevie shook his head, looked at Eva and saw just how fucked up she appeared to be feeling.

He then rushed over to her and gently placed his hand on her left shoulder.

"We're going to find Glen," he said in a soft tone.

Eva stared off into space and slowly nodded her head. Her mind was so far gone that nothing was even processing in her brain at this point.

As Stevie stood over Eva trying to comfort her, they suddenly heard something on the news that caught their attention.

"A man was found murdered outside of an apartment complex in Spring Texas. Due to the severity of the incident, officers are still trying to piece together exactly what happened."

Eva stared at the black male news reporter with a shocked look on her face, and when she saw the clip of Glen's black Mercedes, she suddenly heard loud screaming. It was so loud that her ears were ringing.

Eva was having the craziest out-of-body experience that she didn't even realize that she was the one screaming.

"Oh, my God!" she cried out.

Seeing the same make and model of her husband's car was gut twisting and unbelievable.

"Wow," Evelyn mumbled under her breath as she stared at the flat screen TV with horror in her eyes.

Stevie too was staring at the TV with a shocked look on his face trying to figure out if what the news was reporting held some truth.

Eva's heart was burning, and her vision was blurry. It was like she was in the twilight zone.

She no longer needed confirmation because it was clear as day that the vehicle that she was staring at was Glen's. The only thing she wanted to know now was where the hell his body was.

The next morning, Eva was greeted by two detectives at Evelyn's house.

She was so drained, she couldn't stand up straight. She had large bags under her eyes, and her hair was a mess. She hadn't eaten or showered since the day her husband went missing.

While Eva stood at the door staring at the two black detectives like she was possessed, Evelyn and Stevie stood next to her, trying to comfort her.

"Ma'am, we need you to try to identify the body, if you can," one of the detectives said with a sympathetic look in his eyes.

"Try?" Stevie interrupted.

The detective sighed and slowly nodded his head as if he wasn't being one hundred percent honest about what he knew.

Eva continued to stand still without saying anything because it was like the grim reaper came in and snatched her soul from her body, taking away her ability to see, hear, and think. She was like a zombie. Evelyn looked at the detectives, nodded her head, and closed the door in their faces. Her main focus was sitting her sister down, so that they could all think clearly.

"Come on, sis," she whispered as she sat her down on the sofa.

Eva was so cried out that even if she wanted to break down, she wouldn't be able to produce anymore tears. She was like an empty shell waiting to be washed away. As far as she was concerned, she didn't need to go down to the morgue and identify her husband because her heart was telling her that he was gone. Three hours after the detectives arrived at Evelyn's house, both she and Eva took the long trip to the morgue.

Although Eva felt empty inside and could no longer weep, her heart was starting to tighten. The same anxiety that you get from going high up on a rollercoaster that's getting ready to drop down at a high speed was the same type of anxiety that Eva was feeling.

Going to the morgue was the roller coaster climbing hundreds of feet in the air and identifying her husband's lifeless body would be the terrifying fall. As they stood at the door, Eva held Evelyn's hand so tight, she was cutting off her circulation. It was like getting strapped into the electric chair and waiting for death because Glen's death was the same feeling as Eva dying.

Finally, the mortician came to the door, and when he opened it, he had a straight poker face. His pale white and wrinkled skin was so scary looking it made the experience even more terrifying. Eva squeezed Evelyn's hand even tighter, and when they walked into the room, it was so cold it gave both of them chills. Not knowing who was the wife, due to the fact that Eva and Evelyn were identical twins, the mortician stared at them with a confused look on his face.

Eva still couldn't seem to speak up, so she just stepped a few inches closer to him. He slowly nodded his head and walked over to the table where a large green bag was placed on top of it. Tears then started to fill Eva's eyes, and she was shaking uncontrollably. The feeling was just too surreal, and this was the moment that the roller coaster was about to drop.

The mortician walked over to the bag, slowly unzipped it all the way down, and when he opened it, Evelyn gasped and covered her mouth. Eva stared at the nicely built body that was resting inside of the bag and knew instantly that it was her husband's. The only problem was that he was missing his head...

THE FUCKERY:
LOVING AN INMATE
Author Danielle Bigsby

That jailhouse love... Boy, I tell you, it'll surely suck the life out of you. Loving a man behind bars places your heart on guard. It's easy to fall for their lines and game when they know just what to say. Courting you with letters full of poetic bliss, only to turn around and send those same exact words to the next bitch. Keeping your phone full of Global Tel Link, just so he can ask you the same tired questions every single day. "What did you do today? Do you miss me? Are you going to hold me down out there in the streets?"

Night after night, you're cradling the phone for dear life as you recite, "Baby, I love you and I'm not going anywhere. I'm not like those other girls you had before me. I'm your ride or die." Sinisterly, he's plotting, while hoping to catch you up in a lie. Trying so hard to guilt you into doing whatever he asks.

He has no filter when it comes to asking for exactly what he wants. While you're busy attempting to prove your loyalty, and keeping his books full of your hard-earned money, he's continually asking for more. He desires, better yet claims, to need a cellphone to handle his business, but in the back of your mind you're thinking, *who in the hell is going to call?*

He's not going anywhere any time soon, yet he insists that he's got to have it. While your mind screams for you to avoid this trap at all costs, your heart is like putty in his hands. Just like a dummy, you throw caution to the wind. This fool got your ass doing some dumb shit once again. Reluctantly, you agree, only to find out it's going to cost you three hundred dollars and he's screaming that he needs it right away! So, like a child eagerly attempting to please their parents, you head over to the bank. Withdrawing funds that you know you don't have. Putting yourself in the hole just to prove a point.

Fulfilling his needs has become your new full-time job as his woman. You've convinced yourself that it's your duty and it doesn't matter that he's not free. Holding him down is your way of proving your loyalty. In your mind, he's the king and regardless of his current state, you're still willing to submit.

Now he's got a phone and looking like a heavyweight in jail, while you're robbing Peter to pay Paul. Your family tells you that you're stupid day after day, but your heart tells you that you're in love, so you stay. At this point, loving an inmate has you looking real dumb. As if your situation isn't bad enough, his requests have now escalated to even riskier behaviors. He wants you to risk it all just to prove your loyalty and love.

You're already paying both his cellphone bill and yours every month, but his next request really shakes you up. He's decided that he needs to be the man behind bars. He must make his own money because according to him, he's living beneath his means.

Upon hearing these thoughts, your intuition screams, "What the hell does this nigga need money for? Has he forgotten that he's in jail?"

Your mind says this nigga's crazy, but your heart's a sucker for love, soaking up everything he says while contemplating his retarded ideas. "Baby, I just need a little help from you. I promise that I would never put you in harm's way, but you're the only one I truly trust." Those words fill your heart with glee. Finally hearing him acknowledge that he needs you cements your role in his life, or at least it does in your mind. While he's saying that he needs you, he's filling you full of lies because his true intentions are only to manipulate you.

He doesn't truly want you. He knows that you will do anything he wants, because being represented as a ride or die chick is far too important to you. You can't have other girls in the neighborhood making a move on your position because you can't seem to hold down your man. Such foolish mentality, but it's the street code you live by. Under no circumstances will you have them thinking that you're not a ride or die! Now that he knows you're down, he proceeds to lay out his plan. "Baby, the only way for me to ease the load for you is to tap into this money circulating back here behind these walls. The only thing I need for you to do is make a few deliveries and drop offs. Now, I know that you're nervous, but I promise to walk you through every step. Your hands will never touch drugs directly, because I care about you too much to put you in danger like that. Just a few deliveries to get me established in this game. Don't get quiet on me, baby. Tell me what you think."

Your mind is racing. You can't believe the things that he's just asked of you, but how can you say no to your boo? Not sure of how you should respond to his request, you nervously ask, "Who will I be making deliveries to? On second thought, I don't want to know who I'm going to be delivering this stuff to, but I do want to know how the hell you expect all of this to play out. Do you actually have a plan or are you just going off a whim?"

Knowing that he has to be careful with his words, he delicately replies, "The less you know, the better, baby. It's my job to look out for us as well as protect you from danger, so leave all of the worrying to me, boo." You sigh deeply while contemplating your options.

The Fuckery: Loving an Inmate

On one hand, you'll be proving your loyalty to your man but on the other hand, you'll be going against your morals while literally putting your life on the line. Again, you sigh deeply as you begin to voice your thoughts aloud. "If I choose to do this for you, how can you guarantee me that I won't get caught and if I do get caught, what will happen to me? Will I go to jail? I've never been to jail, baby. How will you be able to protect me then?" Your questions come one after another as your fear becomes apparent.

In that instant, he knows that he's won you over. The questions you ask only give him the reassurance needed to know that you're down for anything, just to prove your loyalty. With broken promises to shield you from any consequences and repercussions, you reluctantly agree to his plan. Within two weeks, he's wasted no time placing you knee deep in the jailhouse drug trade. He's had you picking up drugs and delivering them to prison guards, all the while risking your future for a few dollars on a Green Dot prepaid card. In your mind, the means don't justify the ends, but you can't seem to let go of that street code. Holding down your man is all you know even if it isn't beneficial to you.

He's shelling you out crumbs compared to what he's making behind bars, yet he's telling you that he's barely making it. His clientele is steadily growing, causing him to put more pressure on you to supply him with even more drugs. The deliveries have now gone from once a week to one every two days. Your hands have touched everything, from loose tobacco to Suboxone Strips and you had no idea. Since you didn't originally want to know what you were transporting, he decided to always keep it that way. Your foolishness allowed him to manipulate you without even breaking a sweat but as the pressure to keep the drugs flowing began to mount, he had no choice but to step his game up.

"Baby, I appreciate the risks that you've been taking for us. I'm in here grinding hard to try and take the load off you, but for it to work fully; I'm going to need a little more help from you. I hate to ask anything else of you, considering what you're already doing, but you're the only one that I truly trust with my business." To further guilt you into doing just what he wants, he adds, "I was going to ask my cellie's girlfriend's sister to help me, but I know that you don't want any other woman doing your job."

He already knew that his last statement would only add insult to injury, causing you to say yes before you had a chance to think it all the way through. You can't see him grinning sinisterly, but he is because everything is going according to his plan. What you don't know is that he's already acquired his cellmate's girlfriend's sister as another member of his arsenal. She's receiving just as many "I love you's" as you do, on the phone that you're paying the bill on. Telling her that he's the man behind bars while sending her your hard-earned money. Filling with promises of a fairy tale romance once he's released from jail as he strings you along.

Here you are risking your life and he's busy telling the next bitch that she's going to be his wife. You've now become an expendable pawn in his game and he must find a way to get rid of you without losing the game. In his mind, his cellmate's girlfriend has way more to offer him than you ever possibly could, so he no longer has any use for you. After much contemplation, he finally comes up with the perfect plan and sets it in motion. Just like any other night before, he calls to check up on you. The only difference is that this time his voice is laced full of panic and alarm. "Hey, baby. What's good with you tonight?"

Smiling at the sound of your baby's voice, you reply, "Nothing much, baby. The same old routine sitting here thinking of you. What's good with you? You don't sound like yourself tonight. Is something wrong?" He huffs and puffs to enhance his theatrics and keep you awaiting his response. Unable to hide your anticipation, you begin firing off questions.

"What's wrong, baby? What happened? Did somebody do something to you in there? Did they hurt you, baby? Did the police find your stash? Talk to me, baby. Tell me something, please!" He smiles inwardly, because he has once again suckered you in without much of an effort.

"Ok, baby. I didn't want to tell you this because I don't want you to worry, but I've gotten myself into some mess. I tried my best not to come to you with it, but I have no other choice. The guard that I had you delivering the packages to has messed around and gotten fired. I don't know what I'm going to do now because he was the one bringing the work to me in here. I need you now more than ever, baby." His words hit you like a ton of bricks. How can he be asking you for anything else? You're already giving more than you have to offer, so you can't fathom what he could possibly want now. "Baby, how did the guard get caught up in the first place, and what are you needing me to do now? You know that I love you, but lately you've been asking for a lot of stuff. My bank account is in the red trying to keep all your bills paid, while you're in jail with free rent and three free meals a day.

You have no worries in there, so you spend other people's money like it's water. Your Global Tel Link phone account is full of my hard-earned dollars, just so that you can call three times a day and ask me the same damn questions! Not to mention, that your books are full too. Plus, I'm risking my life for you to live like the rich and famous while I'm struggling just to keep gas in my car! So, with all of this, tell me how I can give any more than I already am?"

Taken aback by your response, he must adjust himself. "Baby, I didn't mean to offend you. I know that I put a lot on you, but it's only because I know that you can come through for me. I wouldn't ask you to do something that I didn't think you were capable of. The load is heavy right now but if you follow my lead just one more time, we'll have more than enough money to ease your mind. I have a plan and you'll be taking a serious risk, but if you do just as I say, you won't have to worry anymore. All I need for you to do is trust me."

Irritated by his incessant beating around the bush, you finally ask, "Baby, what the hell do you want me to do?"

Noticing your agitation, he lays out his plan. "Since the guard got fired, I need you to start packing up the drugs and bringing them in for me, baby. Everything will be dropped off to you with instructions to prepare for our next visit. Just make sure you pack it up real nice and tight, so it'll be easy for you to get it in." His plan left you feeling skeptical but the sound of no longer struggling is appealing to you. You only have one question that needs to be answered.

Where the hell are you supposed to put the package to bring it in? Instead of trying to figure it out on your own, you decide to ask, "Baby where am I supposed to hide the pack until I get inside?"

Laughing, he responds, "Baby, where do you think?"

Still confused, you reply, "Baby, I don't know. Just tell me."

He sighs before replying, "You're really going to make me say it, huh? Ok, baby. It goes inside you. That's why I told you that you're going to have to pack it up real tight. It's going to have to fit up inside your pussy like a dildo. That's the only way it's going to work." If only he could see your face through the phone. What the hell does he mean "it goes inside of you?" What if the drugs leak out? How wide does he think your pussy is? So many questions run through your mind as you try to process the many emotions that you're feeling. You've never been more afraid in your life but if you want to stay afloat, this is your only option. So, you agree to do what he's asking, like a fool.

You're blinded by the money while ignoring the consequences. All week, you practice packing up the drugs until it's taped up just right, making sure that it glides in and out of you with the ease of a tampon. At this point, you're confident and ready. The weekend has come and it's time for you to do what has been asked of you. You go through the proper procedures for visitation and everything goes off without a hitch. You make it up to the visiting room with biggest smile on your face as you await your man's presence. He walks in cool, calm and collected as he spots you seated at the table.

Taking his seat, he smiles and says, "Hey, baby. I'm glad you made it." Beaming with joy, you return his smile and a conversation begins to blossom. Right when you get to the juicy part, he says, "Alright, baby, it's time. Do it exactly like we rehearsed on the phone. Don't get nervous when you go in there. Just do it with one quick motion and come on back out here."

Nervously looking around to make sure no one is watching, you get up and head to the bathroom, also known as the stash spot. Once inside, you head to the nearest stall to get a feel for your surroundings. In the process, you sit on the toilet as if you're using the restroom, so as not to appear suspicious while sliding out your package. Once the coast is clear, you pull up your panties and make a dash for the stash spot along the wall. The package is cuffed in your hands as you pop the lever on the baby's changing table with your left hand, while wedging the package in with your right hand. You know that your time is limited, so you begin to panic and rush no longer thinking about your surroundings, you just want the job done. So, you turn your back to the door while forcing the package in with every ounce of strength you possess.

Finally, you've gotten it all in and you're elated, but just as you go to slide the lever back in place, a problem awaits. All you hear is, "What are you doing?" Frozen in place, you can't think of anything to say except, "Nothing."

What more could you say? You're literally caught red-handed. Fear and shock encompass your face as you wonder what's going to happen next. The last few months play back in your head and suddenly, you're filled with regret. How could you have been so foolish as to get caught up in some mess like this? You had so much going for yourself and now it looks like you'll be heading to jail. To make matters worse, there's no telling how much time you'll face due to the number of drugs you brought in. That package had everything in it, ranging from tobacco, marijuana, powder cocaine, to heroin and crystal meth. In an instant, your whole life has changed because you chose to love an inmate.

You've become a criminal while chasing a false notion of love. To add insult to injury; you find out while locked up that the same man you pledged your love to, was the very one who set you up. He needed you out the way so that he could be on to the next one. So, as you sit in jail fighting for your freedom while trying to mend your broken heart, you finally realize that loving an inmate doomed you from the start, because all he did was manipulate your mind and play with your heart.

The moral of this story is to know your role, because loving an inmate will leave you feeling fucked and not in the right hole.

MY LITTLE SECRET
Jevonne

Zara

You know that we shouldn't be doing this, right?" I asked as we both stripped our clothes off, giving each other kisses.

"It is something about you that I got to have," he responded. "Ever since that night I tasted your lips, I just had to have your body. Watching you at work and all I do is imagine pleasing you and have you riding this dick."

After he rolled the condom down his shaft, I quickly hopped on his erect member and slowly worked my way down, making sure that he touched every inch of my walls. I wanted to have all of him in me and I was determined to have it. Soft moans escaped his mouth as I worked my hips as I lowered myself. He took my breast and put it in his mouth and sucked on it like his life depended on it. Once I had all of him in me, I kissed him like there was no tomorrow.

Our tongues danced and got to know each other as if they never met before. He thrusted upwards in me and it felt so damn good that I started to shudder. I rolled and ground my hips a little faster to ensure that I did have all of him. He started to bounce me up and down and the sound of my juices and my ass hitting on him caused me to tense a little because I feared that someone would hear us and come into the room.

"Baby, slow down, someone might hear us," I said in a whisper.

"I can't, you feel too damn good right now," he responded as he brought me down hard on him. "No, bend me over," I insisted and he gladly obliged. "Oh shit!"

He forcefully thrust in me, hard enough that I had to put my hands on the wall to brace myself. He held onto my hips and picked up the pace. I threw it back on him and made my ass clap like the strippers do at Onyx.

I heard him say, "Yes baby, just like that. Throw that ass back for me."

That only boosted my ego a little bit more and I started to work him as if he was my man, Eric. Don't get it twisted, I love Eric, but lately he's been lacking. At first, when I met Kerry, I knew he was no good for me. Even though I found him very attractive, I noticed how he talked to the other women at the job. Granted, he's been working here longer than I have, so it's only right that he has built a rapport with them. What made it different was in his delivery. It seemed like he was flirting and in hindsight, he may have been doing just that and might have had some of them in this same position I'm in right now.

"Fuck," I let out as he thrust harder, bringing me out of my thoughts. He kept up the hard thrusts but now they were quicker, which told me he's near his climax. I decided to capitalize on that fact and tighten my muscles around his dick. He instantly gripped my waist for dear life and dug deeper in me. I bounced on the tip of his dick as he tried to push in further and that shit drove him crazy that after the fourth time, I let him push right in and let his children fill the condom and I let all of my juices lubricate his pelvis.

"Damn baby, I knew you had some good ass pussy," he said as he pulled out and gave me a kiss on the back of my neck.

"I could say the same about your dick game," was the only thing that I could think of to say. He came to me and kissed me with so much passion, I was ready to go another round. It was as if he was thinking the same thing, because I felt him get hard again and it began to jump. I unwillingly stopped kissing him and pushed him off of me with some force, because of his resistance.

"Uh-uh, we can't go another round. We've been gone long enough and my break is nearly up," I said in a hurry as I got my clothes on.

I thought, *how did Kerry and I get to this point?* No matter how much I curved him, he kept coming back. It was like he was determined to have me, and now he has succeeded in his quest.

"So, no more morning and goodnight texts and all of the lovey-dovey messages, huh?" I said as flatly as I could, knowing that I didn't want to know the answer.

"Why would you say that?" he asked.

"Because we both know this can't go beyond what we just did," I reminded him.

"You think that I'm letting you go after you just put it on me the way you did?" he said without getting too loud.

"Hell no, you mines now and I don't care about what you say about your man. Fuck him, he just lost a gem."

"Oh, fuck him, huh? And what about you? You claiming me, and you got a woman? Are you saying fuck her too? May I also remind you that she can walk in this room at any moment, so move so I can get back to my office," I responded, pushing him out of my path.

I walked down the hall and nearly ran into Aisha. "Hey Aisha," I said loud enough for him to hear me, hoping that he would get the signal. "I'm so sorry, I didn't see you there. You good, do you need help with anything?" I hoped making small talk would buy me some time for other people to start walking onto the hall.

"Yeah, I'm good. I'm 'bout to go on lunch," she responded.

"Do you want me to get you anything while I'm out?"

"Oh, nah, I'm good. See you when you get back." As I continued down the hall to my office, I was thinking, *I had what I wanted already*. As I settled in my chair, guilt washed over me as I looked at my wedding photo of my husband and I. Eric is a good man, but I can't trust him anymore. Honestly, I don't why I'm still with him but in a weird way, this thing between Kerry and I made me want Eric more sexually. Come to think of it, our marriage has become less sex and even less communication or anything else, as a matter of fact. We hardly spend anytime anymore and he's been on his phone more secretly, or so he thinks.

I peeped game though and haven't said anything about it, because eventually what he's doing will all come out. Now I don't feel so guilty anymore for what I just did. I looked up from my desk as Kerry passed by and he blew me a kiss. I instantly blushed and reached for my phone. Knowing that I shouldn't be doing what I'm about to do, I still did it anyway. About fifteen minutes later, he was in my office with his tools. I got up and opened the blinds to my office and closed the door. By the time I turned around, he was already behind my desk on the floor.

I sat down as if everything was normal, parting my legs just enough for him to rub his fingers around my clit. As he applied pressure, I moved my hips in a circle, then he slowly slipped his finger through my wetness and played with my box. He added another finger and started to inch deeper into my cavern of wetness. I slowly began to open my legs wider and he gladly obliged and gave me his tongue.

The instant our lips met, I gave way to a small squirt of my juices for him to taste. He dipped his tongue in and began to suck as if it was his favorite drink and he just couldn't get enough. I tried my hardest to keep a straight face while holding the phone to my ear, until he started sucking on my clitoris. I leaned back in my chair and he pulled me closer and got deeper. I took my free hand and pushed his head deeper as I released everything I had in me.

"Kerry, Keh-Keh, oh shit!"

"Damn baby, I need this every day," he said, cleaning his face off.

"No, this wasn't even supposed to go down like this. We could lose our jobs, especially me. Plus, you know I'm married."

"That ain't got nothing to do with me, but let me get back out here. I'll see you out in the shed before you leave, right?"

"Uh no, you just got that down there," I said, laughing.

The next morning, I had my good morning message from Kerry, but this time it was a video message. He was in the bathroom taking care of himself, saying that he wished it was me that was helping him take care of his morning wood. Usually, I'm not a big fan of videos like this, but this one turned me on. I quickly saved it to my phone for later. The morning started out with my husband being quiet and unaffectionate, as usual. Given the way Kerry made me feel with that video, I tried to have a little foreplay with Eric, but it was to no avail.

The most I got was a kiss before he left for work, not even an "I love you" or an "I want you later" look. I stood there in my blue lace boy short set in front of my full-length mirror and looked myself over to see if I could see what Eric doesn't see in me anymore. I stood at 5'5", size 40-DD breasts, 30-inch waist, and 44-inch hips. My side profile revealed a butt resembling a cut-in-half honeydew melon that every man gawked at and would love to feel on if given the chance.

My skin was chocolate brown and had a few blemishes here and there, but nothing grotesque, just bad acne. I even grew locs for him that are now touching my mid-back. Physically, I was a perfect catch for any man. I took a few pics of myself at different angles, even one with me bent over looking back at it. I sent a few to Kerry and even decided to send the same ones to Eric.

We used to do things like this, but then stopped. I hoped that this would put a spark in him to get things back on track with us. Morning meetings seem to take forever. Eric never responded to my messages, which only made me my suspicions about him cheating on me more believable. At least someone appreciated my pics; Kerry messaged me during morning meeting, saying that he needed to have me again today and at this point, I'm considering it. Walking the halls and doing my rounds on my patients, I decided to act on the need to be held, touch, and feel wanted.

Me: I'll get a room after work.

Kerry: I was getting worried that you would turn me down.

Me: Can you stay the night with me?

Kerry: I'll see what I can do.

Reading those words sent a spark through me. I swear, if Kerry wasn't involved or whatever he calls it with his girlfriend, I would replace him with Eric. What am I thinking? The grass ain't always greener on the other side. I can't do this with Kerry, what was I thinking? I got back to my office and began on some reports for the nurses when a knock came at my door.

"Hey baby, are you busy?" he said, stepping into my office.

I was shocked to say the least. I asked, getting up from behind my desk, "Eric, what are you doing here?"

"I want to apologize to you and I didn't want to wait until we both got home to do so," he said, hugging me. "Can you leave early and let's get a jump on the weekend? I have a surprise for you." I saw Kerry starring at us through my office window. It would be my luck that Eric came to his senses after I made plans with Kerry. It was like he had a sixth sense.

"Apologize for what?" I questioned him, acting as if I didn't have a clue.

"What did you do?"

"This morning, you was, well...you know and the pictures you sent, and I didn't respond. I'm sorry and I know I haven't been showing you my love like I used to, and I'm going to change that by starting today," he went on.

"Uh, excuse me, Mrs. Watson," Kerry said, knocking on my door. "Is this a good time to come and finish what I started yesterday on your desk?"

"Oh, hey Kerry, ummm...not right now," I said. "I'm staying in for lunch, so maybe after I leave today or tomorrow."

"Why don't we do like I suggested? Let the man finish the work in your office and let's go," Eric asked.

"Baby, I can't," I stated. "We are getting ready for state and I got to make sure that the nurses are in compliance. I have a lot of paperwork to do and go through. I may even be home late tonight." He sighed.

"Well, can you at least go to lunch with me then, since I'm already over this way?"

"Sure," I responded. "You can go ahead, Kerry."

"Actually, I got to take care of something else first," he said, exiting the office. I searched my husband's face to see if he picked up a vibe from Kerry, and he was easy to read like a book.

"What is up with him?" he asked.

Gathering my things, I countered, "What do you mean?"

"First, he came in wanting to finish up whatever he was doing in here and when you told him he could, he declined," he stated.

"I don't know, hun. He did say that he had something else to do first," I said, not trying to sound guilty. "Why you worried about that for?"

"I saw him passing back and forth your office looking in, before I came in," he answered. "How well do you know him?"

"Eric, please don't do this," I started. "Not at my job. I like to keep a drama-free work place and keep my personal and professional life separate."

"Just answer my question," he demanded. "If there is nothing to hide, just be truthful."

I sighed. "Here we go. Okay, fine. I don't know him that well. He is friendly to all the female staff here. He has flirted with me in the past when I first started to work here, but I shut it down and it is no longer an issue. His girlfriend is one of the nurses here. Satisfied?"

"No, but since you say you handled it, I'm going to leave it at that," he stated as we exited my office. While at lunch with Eric, Kerry kept blowing up my phone, to the point that I had to turn it off so that Eric wouldn't get suspicious. We actually had a decent conversation and a good lunch. We even got a quickie in before I went back to work. All of that couldn't erase or make up for the months he's been ignoring me. As the day went on, Eric kept texting me lovely memes and wanting to make plans for trips. It seemed like he was forcing something, but all on my mind was on was seeing Kerry after work. I didn't see Kerry for the rest of the day and he never answered any of my messages. I hope he wasn't mad that I didn't answer him while I was with Eric at lunch.

I did a lil shopping for some lingerie before I came to the hotel room. I don't know why, but I wanted tonight to be different. I didn't want the "just hit it and leave" sex with him. After forty-five minutes of waiting, I started to think that I was being stood up. I texted and called Kerry again and it was to no avail. I waited about ten more minutes and then began to pack up to leave. As I opened the door, Kerry was standing outside against the balcony.

"Why are you standing out here, why haven't you come in?" I asked. He just stood there looking at me.

"Kerry, is everything alright? Talk to me, say something."

"I can't do this," he started.

"Are you serious, Kerry?" I exclaimed. "You got me up in here waiting and then want to say that you can't do this! You got me here jeopardizing my marriage and *you* can't do this!"

"I mean, I can't sneak around, Zara; I want us to be together," he said as my mouth dropped open.

"You want what?" I stuttered in shock. "Come inside and let's talk, because you are talking crazy. What do you mean; you want to be with me?"

"I mean, I want to have a relationship with you. I want you as my woman," he said, pulling me close to him and removing the bag from my shoulder.

"Seeing you with your husband today made me realize that I am what you need. I can treat you the way that you are supposed to be treated and not taken for granted, like he does."

"Kerry, we discussed this before, we can't be together," I stated.

"This was only to be for us to get it out of our system and then maybe every now and again."

"Zara, look I told Aisha tonight that it is over between us and that I will be moving out soon," he said. "She didn't take it well, but I need to cut ties with her so that I can be with you."

"You did what?" I exclaimed.

"Why would you do something so stupid, Kerry! Okay, okay, Kerry look, let's think this through and I mean, really think this through. Now I have been married to Eric for three years and yes, we've had our ups and downs, but I love him and I won't leave him. We barely know each other outside of work, and this wouldn't even last a month if we did give it a try. So let's just go back to what we agreed on in the first place. Just sex and nothing more."

"I know that we would be good together, just give us a chance, Zara," he pleaded. I sat on the bed, racking my brain over and over to see if I wanted to go down this road. What the hell am I thinking! I can't go down this road; it is only going to cause hurt, pain, and a lot of turmoil. I can't leave my husband for a fling that might not go anywhere. Yeah, he most likely has been cheating on me, but two wrongs don't make a right. Then again, I've always been the good one, the one that is always taking the higher road and still gets shitted on in the end. On the other hand, I could use Kerry to my own advantage and string him along and when I get tired of him, make him not want to be with me anymore.

"Ok, this is how it going to happen until we can finally be in the open about us. We will continue to meet after work, here, but we will have to watch ourselves at work," I demanded.

"Fine, what about on the phone?" he asked. "Do we have to stop texting?"

"No, we can still text, but watch the time that you do text. I don't want Eric to get suspicious of anything before everything is finalized. I will find a divorce lawyer and see if I can find any proof that Eric has cheated on me, so that will make the divorce process easier," I added.

"Okay. Now do you have to leave right now?" he asked, in between giving me kisses on my neck while caressing my ass.

"Mmmm...yes I do," I moaned.

"Not yet, please," he begged.

"Kerry...uh, come on," I let out.

"I got to get home before he starts calling and texting me."

"I don't care, you're mines now and I want you," he whispered in my ear.

At this point, my bags were already on the floor and I started to undo his pants quickly. My head was telling me to stop, but everything else said no. Within the next hour we had, well after round three, I stopped counting. I noticed it was about 11:45 and texted Eric to let him know that I stopped over at my mom's place for a while. I was a bit surprised not to find a missed call from him. I gathered my things and left before Kerry could wake up. I left him a note and the key to check out when he got up.

When I got home, Eric's car wasn't in the driveway. Once inside, I noticed nothing has been moved or touched and even our bed had no signs of having been slept in. I checked my phone to see if he replied to my text and nothing. I showered and went to bed. I checked my phone one last time, before calling it a night and still nothing. It wasn't like Eric to not respond to my messages or just call to check in.

His behavior is a total 180 from how he was earlier today. I just prayed that nothing was wrong with him and that he was okay.

CHAPTER 2

ERIC

Now I get to tell y'all my side of things. I know my wife probably made it out like I treat her like she is nothing or worthless, but that is far from the truth. I love my wife, she is my God send. When we met, it was a time in my life where I didn't want to settle down, but I knew I couldn't let her get away and become someone else's wife. So, I did what I had to do to keep her and make her fall in love with me. Yes, I still kept other women on the side, but I didn't love any of them. Zara will forever have my heart, but I don't think I'm ready to give up these other women yet. I'm careful with what I do and I always wrap it up and come home to Zara. Well, not tonight; tonight I think I have made the biggest mistake that will cost me to lose Zara for good.

After having lunch with Zara, I got a call from Cherise, saying that it is important that we meet ASAP. So, here I am, laid up in this hotel room with her.

"I got to go, Cherise," I said, looking at the ceiling with her head on my chest. "Zara is probably..."

"Seriously, Eric?" she puffed. "I just told you that we are going to have a baby and we made love; not once, but twice and now you're telling me about your wife? Hmph, fine. Go. Run home to your boring wife and boring life."

"Come on, Cherise, I don't need this right now. We agreed that the last time was the last time and I was going to do right by my wife," I said.

"Also, we are not having a baby. You are going to have an abortion and then we are going to go our separate ways."

"The hell I am," she jumped up yelling.

"I ain't having no damn abortion! I'm keeping our child and that is that. Whatever you need to tell wifey, you do that, but I'm not having an abortion."

I got up and started to get dressed. "Cherise, right now...look, I hate to tell you this, but the only person I'm having children with is my wife. I'm sorry, but if you keep this baby, I will have nothing to do with it."

"Oh wow," she exclaimed.

"Just a few moments ago, you were telling me that you love me and you made a mistake about cutting me off, and now that I'm pregnant and keeping our child, you don't want nothing to do with us! Baby, this is what we talked about. Having a family one day and now we are presented with the opportunity. You can tell your wife that it's not working or whatever and get a divorce. Then we can be together and raise our child together like a real family."

As Cherise talked, I sat on the bed and listened to her trying to reason with me. I checked my phone to see a message from Zara, saying that she was on her way home from her mom. I didn't even realize that I've been with Cherise that long and there was no way I was going to get home before her. I might as well stay and come up with an excuse in the morning that she will be satisfied with.

In the meantime, I need to get Cherise to calm her ass down and convince her not to go through with this pregnancy. Shit, what am I saying? I need to take my ass home now while there won't be that much of a blowback.

"Are you even listening to me, Eric?" she asked, waving her hand in my face. "Yeah baby, I hear you," I said.

She scoffed, "Now I'm baby? Just a minute ago...man, whatever.

I don't care what you do, but I know what I'm going to do and that is keep my child." I grabbed her and pulled her to the bed.

"Come here with your mean self. I'm sorry. You just caught me off guard and you know it is a lot. Just give me some time to get things straight at home and then we can move forward with what will be the next step. We got some time right before the final decision is made for us, right?"

"Right," she answered.

"Okay then. So stop coming for my head and give me some more...," I hinted. "Stop, E," she giggled as I nibbled on her ear and then moved to her neck.

"Uh-uh, let me go to the bathroom first."

I undressed and laid back in the bed, thinking of what to say to Zara. I texted my buddy, Michael, to give him the heads up, in case Zara contacted him looking for me. Cherise came out the bathroom with nothing but a smile on her face. She had some of the perkiest C-cup breasts that I've seen. They were full and round, actually looked like they were implants, but they didn't compare to my wife's double D's. I am an ass man, but I do love a nice size breast to snuggle my head on while my hands are full with a nice juicy ass.

When I look at Cherise's body, compared to my wife's own, she had nothing compared to her. In that moment, I tried to think about what made me fall for her. My wife was down to do and try anything sexually with me; she didn't stress me out, or bug me with trivial nonsense. I think our communication was okay, but I could talk to Cherise about anything, and I mean anything. There are some things that she knows that my wife doesn't even know. It's not that my wife isn't easy to talk to, I just don't want her to think...ah, I don't know.

"A penny for your thoughts," she said, while straddling me and kissing on my neck.

"So you just going to go for my spot like that, huh?" I said. She nodded her head. "Okay, well come here then."

"Eric," she yelled as I flipped her over. I kissed and licked her neck while my hands caressed her body. I slowly moved my way down between her thighs. I kissed, licked, and bit the sensitive part of her inner thighs over and over. She tried to inch away, but I kept pulling her back to me. I felt the heat resonating from between her legs every time I go near her cavern. I gave her small pecks and licked the small trail of juices that were already escaping her. Hearing her moans and watching her body react to my touch made me want to...

"Yes, baby," she moaned. "Please eat it."

I shook my head and rubbed my nose against her cavern in the process. I know she can't stand being teased and it only builds up her intensity of wanting it more. She squirmed beneath me and tried to push my head further. Eventually, I gave her what she wanted. Had her screaming and calling out my name like she was praising God. Each time she dug her nails into my back or left a scratch, I went deeper and harder. I took my frustration of this whole situation with her out on her. It was like I want to fuck the baby out of her and make this whole situation go away.

"Eric, slow down," she panted. "Eric! B-b-b-baby!"

I squeezed around her neck a little tighter every time she called my name. Her eyes became huge as if she'd just realized what I was trying to do to her. Her eyes showed it all for her; her life, character, and whatever she wanted you to see. It was all in her eyes and now those same eyes were losing life, becoming dull and soon nonexistent; along with her body that became still beneath me.

Jevonne

ENGAGED TO A MARRIED WOMAN
Author Fanita Moon Pendleton

The Brent's

Lavish parties are a custom in high society. They are a time for women to show off their designer gowns, and men of power to make deals all under the umbrella of champagne flutes and crystal chandeliers. Waiters in tuxedos smoothly worked the room, ensuring all the guests had drinks. The eighteen-piece band delighted the crowd with sounds from the Jazz Age.

It was a celebration; the occasion was a fundraiser for Justin Brent's bid in the Senate race. People were falling over themselves to be a part of the Brent Political Dynasty. Justin's father was Congressman Joshua Brent and his grandfather, rest his soul, was the beloved Speaker of The House, Jordan Brent.

You might say patriotism ran deep in the Brent family. The historic John Marshall Ballroom was filled to capacity, with a who's who in the political world and a roster of superstars clamoring to pay 50,000 dollars a plate to be a part of history. It was said when a Brent decides to run for office, American flags everywhere fly a little higher; they were loved by all.

Justin was not the only Brent making headlines. His twin brother, Austin, decided he would be better suited to run the family business; Brent Electrical. The latest Brent Electrical patent is the technology behind the electrical car. The company has always been on the cutting edge and five steps above the competition.

With Austin running the company revenue was through the roof with 16.999 billion dollars; earning Brent Electric a top spot on the Fortune 500. Last year, profits were over thirteen million and counting. Between politics and business, the Brent's were golden.

Justin and Austin were twenty-nine years old. They looked more like models than a politician and a CEO, standing 6'3" with a strong and solid 200-pound frame. Most women say their best features are their gray eyes and curly blond hair. Of the two, Justin was the most comfortable in his skin. He embodied the Hollywood sex symbol style. They clearly took their looks from their mother, Julia Brent. She was the real backbone of the Brent family. A statuesque blonde with Hollywood glamour, there wasn't a camera alive that didn't love Julia and when they were young, Julia never missed an opportunity to have the Brent twins in the limelight. She believed they single-handedly captured the heart of America, and in turn, votes for their father's Congress run. The twins excelled in academics, attending all the finest prep schools.

They both were top of their class at Princeton, Austin graduating summa cum laude and Justin right behind him, obtaining magna cum laude in business. The original plan was for the twins to take over the family business from their aging uncle, Barnacle Brent. He had been grooming them both since they were teenagers. Their father was a CEO in name only; he left all business decisions to his brother. Barnacle was unable to have any children of his own, so his nephews were his legacy for the company his father built.

He was initially hurt by Justin's decision to leave the company and follow behind his father and enter politics, but the reality was politics was also a Brent family legacy. The day Austin took over as CEO of Brent Electric was the proudest day of Barnacle's life. The fundraiser was in high gear and Justin and Austin were working the room like the seasoned pros they were, when a woman approached them from the rear. Austin noticed her first.

"Hello, Madeline, and how is your evening?" he said loud enough to catch his brother's attention. Madeline Rowe was a powerful woman who assumed everything belonged to her; including Justin Brent. Raising her glass to the brothers with a twinkle in her eye, Madeline looked at Justin as she answered Austin's question.

"Why, Austin, I am splendid this evening and I just love the accommodations at The Jefferson, don't you?" She never caught the confused look on Austin's face.

But Justin did and laughed slightly, because he knew exactly what Madeline was doing. She was making a halfhearted attempt to tell him where she would be staying, in hopes he would show up and rekindle a fire that had long ago extinguished. Instead of embarrassing her further, Justin said, "Of course, Maddy. The Jefferson is one of the finest places around.

Um, will you excuse us please?" He nudged Austin, who was still behind the eight ball, and told him they needed to go check on that thing. The twins left Madeline to contemplate if Justin using his play name for her was a sign of affection. The night was turning out to be a success. By the amount of people in the room, a ton of money had been raised for the election cause. Austin was standing on the podium, looking noticeably awkward. As he tapped the microphone, the music slowly lowered, causing everyone to give him their attention as he began to speak.

"I want to first thank all of you for coming out to support my twin brother in his bid for the Senate. I never had any doubt he would do wonderful things." There was applause and Justin could be seen in the crowd, waving and smiling like a Cheshire cat as Austin continued. "I have an announcement of my own to make tonight." He clears his throat.

"It's a surprise to everyone, but we wanted to share our news this way." Austin began looking around the stage and gave a nod in the direction of the left corner. She sashayed towards Austin glowing like a sparkling star. Cheers could be heard in the crowd as she made her way over to Austin and kissed him. Camera flashes were flickering as if the young couple were movie stars.

Austin peeled his eyes away long enough to say, "I know most of you already know this beautiful woman standing here with me, but let me re-introduce you to her. I want you all to say hello to Jessica Dublin-Brent, my wife."

A collective gasp and claps were growing in the room. The sound of the applause sounded like the rhythm section of the finest jazz band. Austin made eye contact with both his father and brother, he couldn't tell rather they were happy with his news or pissed, but he continued to speak, going for broke.

"Jessica and I are not only a union in marriage, but we would also like to announce the merger of Brent Electric and Dublin Engineering." With that, the couple kissed again and then walked away from the podium as reporters clamored to speak to them and take their picture. When they made it from the stage, Justin and Joshua Brent were standing there. The look on their faces was indifferent; they have been involved in the public long enough not to give away how they were feeling to a photographer. Austin held Jessica's hand as she stepped from the podium, still smiling for photos.

The band began to play an upbeat tune that caught people's attention and some began to move towards the dance floor, while others went back to discussing what the recent Brent news meant. Austin was in a staring match with his brother and father that was becoming more uncomfortable by the moment, until Jessica stepped in and said, "Why don't we go into the other room and talk? There is no need to continue to stare at each other out here in public."

Joshua was trying to keep his cool when he said, "And why not, missy? You and my son decided to do this out here in public." He was waving his hands around at the crowd of spectators, visibly pissed that Jessica would have the nerve to address him.

Justin stepped up and said, "You know what, she is right. Let's go into the back offices and talk, but I don't want to be gone too long."

The family retreated to the back offices of the ballroom. If steam could be seen, it surely would be seen coming from Joshua Brent. He despised the Dublin family and everything they stood for and both boys damn well knew it. He felt Austin had deliberately spit in his face after everything he did for him. The slamming door alerted everyone to just how pissed the elder Brent was, but his words left no doubt.

"After all I have done for you, you pull this. You marry this black bitch and parade her around at the biggest night of your brother's life?" Joshua was yelling so loud spittle was flying from his mouth, but that didn't stop him from continuing.

"And not only do you marry this tramp, but you link her to my father's business. A business my dad built with his blood, sweat and tears. What the fuck is wrong with you, boy?" Suddenly, there was a loud bang on the table that caused everyone to turn around. What they saw might frighten the average man, but not a Brent; the words she spoke, however, reminded them of the power of a woman

"Now sir and I say that, trying to hold on to the last little bit of respect I have for you. You have called me a black bitch and a tramp and you don't even know the first thing about me, so I can only assume you are a racist, sexist pig. And that's fine, you can be that, but let me assure you as a wife, I am more than Austin deserves and as a business partner, I am the best he will ever have. Now you put that in your pipe and smoke it." Staring at three mystified looks, Jessica walked out of the door to rejoin the party.

Jessica Dublin-Brent was the most powerful woman in the world of engineering. She learned the business from the time she was a teenager, working at Dublin Engineering every summer. She was an only child, never having the brother her father so desperately wanted. But Jessica was very eager to learn and the result was her graduating at the top of her class with a degree in Engineering from Cornell University. She was smart, beautiful, and the sole heir to one of the largest engineering firms in the country.

The fact she was also African American was not a hindrance as far as Jessica was concerned. She knew she earned every honor she ever received. The attraction to Austin had been there for as long as she could remember, but when she mentioned it to her father, he was dead set against her getting involved with anyone with the last name Brent. She could never get a straight answer from him and now she never would, because he died three years ago. Shortly after her father's death, she ran into Austin at a conference and they began seeing each other quietly. They both agreed; keeping their family out of their personal lives would give them a chance to get to know each other without undue outside influence. As she walked back to the party, Jessica was glad they made that decision. It has had its positives and now here come the negatives.

Austin was sitting on the corner of the desk, ready to go to war with his brother and father over his wife. The atmosphere was thick, but they had been here before and made it through.

"So, is someone going to say something, because I have to get back to my fundraiser?" said an impatient Justin.

In his mind, what's done is done. At the end of the day Brent's support Brent's in what they do. He was ready to stand for his brother in his marriage and business decisions. Neither he nor his father was ready to run the family business. Although they were both CEO's on paper, they didn't have the voting power to stop Austin from running the company how he saw fit. In essence, they both just collected checks and did little to no work.

The elder Brent was still visibly upset, but just shook his head at his eldest by two minutes' son and said, "I hope you know what you are doing." The look of disgust on his face was evident as he walked out of the room slamming the door. Austin stood and extended his hand to his brother, saying, "I sure hope I didn't ruin your party, Jus."

Justin started to laugh at his twin. "You could never ruin anything. If your announcement of the merger is good for business, then it's good for the family. And you can marry whoever the hell you want to; forget what Dad is talking about." That's all that Austin needed to hear as the brothers embraced and headed back to the party in better spirits.

Austin watched his wife from across the room; she was marvelous in her curve-hugging black Versace gown. He admired how she captured the room with her splendor, standing 5'9" and packing a powerful 160 pounds of beauty into her dress; she was radiant. Her skin was a shade of brown that reminded him of creamy chocolate. Austin felt like he could look at her for hours and never get tired.

Jessica was three years older than him, but you couldn't tell it by her beauty, enthusiasm for life or her sexual appetite. He knew he made the right decision when it came to Jessica. Walking over and rescuing his wife from an investor from Nafta Pharmaceutical, he could see the relief on her face.

"I must have had the 'I need rescuing' look on my face, dear." The scent of her perfume was driving him wild, he tried to place it; it wasn't too strong but there was a hint of peach and apple. She was causing him to lose concentration without making any effort.

"You had the 'I want to go home and make powerful love to my husband look' on your face and who am I to disappoint?" Austin whispered in her ear, which caused her to blush from ear to ear while she answered.

"That is exactly what I was thinking. Let's go." The couple attempted to leave the ballroom without being spotted, but Justin saw them and called out to them from the group that he was entertaining

"Austin and Jessica, I would like you to meet Monica. Monica, this is my brother, Austin, and his very lovely wife, Jessica."

Greetings were made all around as Justin said, "Monica is thinking about becoming my personal aide, what do you think, Austin?" The smile coming from Monica could have radiated the entire ballroom. Austin wasn't slow on this uptake, so he played along with his twin.

"Well, brother; that depends on what Monica's qualifications are." Shaking his head as if in deep thought, Justin caught a glimpse at Jessica's disapproval just as he said, "I tell you what, twin, I am going to give her an interview and I will let you know if she got the job."

Justin patted Austin on the back and said, "You guys have a good night and congratulations again." Austin and Jessica made their way from the ballroom and waited for their driver to pull up as Austin began to chuckle.

"That brother of mine is something else. He has always been the ladies' man. I can only imagine what type of interview he is going to give that girl."

Jessica saw absolutely nothing funny, but decided to keep it to herself as they got into the black stretch limo and relaxed for the ride back to their Bethesda, Maryland home.

CHAPTER 2

A Forgotten Time

Two days after the fundraiser, Joshua Brent sat in his study in the Beverly Hills section of Alexandria, Virginia, in a somber mood. Looking out the window, he admired his neighborhood for the peaceful life that it afforded him and his wife. However, the tranquil feel of the neighborhood could not squash the utter disgust he felt at his son marrying that Dublin girl. The Brent's feud with the Dublin's is over thirty years old and did not die with Dirk Dublin.

Joshua turned in his chair and stared at a painting of his wife that hung over the fireplace. The painting was lifelike. It was his wife in all her glorious splendor. Julia was smiling back at him from the picture almost mockingly, in her beautiful cream Vera Wang gown that flowed like a wedding dress. Joshua remembered the day the famous painter came to their home to create the masterpiece like it was yesterday. He remembered marveling at his wife's beauty and feeling like the luckiest man alive to have her in his corner.

Not only was she beautiful, but she was a political asset to his family, having come from a large Virginian political family. Joshua stared at the painting and remembered what started the bad blood between the Brent's and the Dublin's.

The winter of 1980 was a brutal one in the Virginia countryside. The Brent family was hunkered down, trying to ride it out like everyone else. Joshua was Senator Brent back then and his father, Jordan, was Speaker of The House, second in line for Presidential succession. Joshua remembered the amount of pressure that he felt being the son of the great Jordan Brent. He strived extra hard to follow in his father's footsteps, unlike his brother, Barnacle, who chose to work in the family business, rather than follow his father into politics.

He snuggled with Julia on the fluffy rug and realized he was thankful for all his blessings. It wasn't until he felt something wet hit his arm that he realized that Julia was crying. His heart instantly ached; he pulled away and asked, "Why are you crying dear?"

Nothing hurt him more than to see her sad. The look on her face was one of pure anguish, she tried to speak, but it only made her break down into tears. Julia leaned into Joshua's shoulder and cried herself to sleep and he held her all night, wondering what could be bothering his wife. The next morning, bright and early, Joshua reached for his wife and she was not in bed. He was immediately concerned after her behavior last night. The sunlight was peeking through the curtains, but he could see that the snow was still falling hard.

Shaking his head at the weather, he grabbed his robe and put on his slippers. A mixture of crying and coughing could be heard coming from the direction of his bathroom. Rushing in that direction, he found his wife hugging the toilet with her head almost at the bottom of it. He immediately ran water in the sink and wet a towel for her.

"Here you go, love. What's wrong with you? Do you want me to call Dr. Rich?"

When Julia came up for air, her eyes were bloodshot red as if she had never stopped crying from the night before. Her normally tamed blonde hair was disheveled and she was shaking her head furiously.

"No, Jo, I don't want a doctor. I don't know what I want anymore." That last statement was perplexing to Joshua; he knelt next to his wife and wiped her face with the cool rag.

His patience and sweet demeanor seemed to have a negative effect on his wife and she became uncharacteristically abusive, screaming,

"Leave. Just leave me alone, Jo. Let me think. Let me breathe, please!"
Joshua had never seen his wife like this and he was scared for her, but
he did as she asked and gave her room to breathe.

Joshua tried to get some work done, but politics were the last
thing on his mind. He was worried sick about his wife, along with
having cabin fever caused by the weather. He sat in his study behind
his vintage oak desk. This desk had been passed down through
generations of Brent men and was one of his most prized possessions.
It made him feel connected to the past and hopeful for the future. He
hoped to one day pass it down to his own son. Joshua ran his hand
across the desk and thought about all the decisions that were made
around the desk, not only by his father, but his grandfather.

The door to his study opened suddenly and in walked Julia. She
looked refreshed; her hair was done and she was dressed as if she was
going to a luncheon in her smart houndstooth skirt and red top. The
sign that things were still not right with her were the redness of her
gray eyes.

She walked towards Joshua, never losing eye contact with him as
she took a seat as if she was there for a scheduled meeting. The
thickness in the air was too much for Joshua. He continued to rub on
the desk as he stared in his wife eyes and said, "Are you ready to tell
me what is going on with you, Julia?"

She cleared her throat already making up her mind; she was
strong enough to get through this. She was a Custis and Custis
women could face any challenge; even this. Holding her head up nice
and strong and sticking her chest out to encourage her speech, she
said, "I am pregnant."

Joshua stopped rubbing the desk as a smile broke out from his
heart to his eyes and he shouted, "That's wonderful, Julia! I am so

excited, oh my God! Why are you crying and sad, this is wonderful news!" He jumped up from his seat to make his way over to his wife; he couldn't remember when he had been so happy.

Before he could make it all the way around the desk she yelled, "It's not yours, Jo.... The baby is not yours!"

The ringing of the phone brought him back from his nightmare. Thinking about that time in his life was more painful than he wanted to admit to anyone. Picking up the phone, he said more forcefully than he planned, "Hello!"

The caller was a reporter with *The Ledger* and wanted to know if he wanted to comment on his son's marriage to Dirk Dublin's daughter. Before Joshua could hang up on him, the reporter went on to comment the rumor mill was saying Dublin was his archenemy and now Dublin's daughter was half-owner of his family's business. Once the reporter came up for air, Joshua took his frustration out on him.

"Your rumor mill knows nothing about my family and I would suggest you get your facts straight, before I sue *The Ledger* and you personally."

He slammed the phone down so hard, it cracked in two places. He was beyond pissed and could feel his pressure rising. He was sixty years old and stress was wreaking havoc on his system, causing him to have heart palpitations.

Joshua looked back out the window of his study and took some slow smooth breaths of air. He could feel his heart regulating just as Julia walked into the room.

"Jo, what are you up to? You have been closed up in here all day." She had her arms folded across her ample chest with a look of annoyance grazing her beautiful features as she continued, "You can't control your children's lives, Jo! Let the past go! And as for Austin, what is done is done!"

With that, Julia turned and stormed right back out of the door. He could hear the pleading in her voice and he promised her years ago he would let it go, but sitting there thirty-three years later, he just wasn't sure if he could anymore.

CHAPTER 3

Round Three

The sun peeking through the blinds didn't stop Justin from indulging in his favorite morning snack as he slowly snaked down through his Merino Egyptian thousand-count cotton sheets. Justin loved to show women his twenty-two carat gold sheets and brag that they were handmade. He didn't need any help in the bedroom, but he loved the look on their face as they contemplated how fast they could remove their clothes to feel those sheets on their body.

Most people assumed that he was a square because he was rich and well educated; it was quite the opposite. Out of the two, Justin was the one who was more laid back and fun to be around. He enjoyed a good joke, loved to hang out with his friends and the ladies, well that was another story. Some consider him the quintessential ladies' man; with his model looks and sexy physique, he never has problems with the ladies. Managing all of this with a professional life in the limelight is a nightmare for his campaign manager.

He has been called everything from the gigolo politician, to the next sex scandal waiting to happen. All of that could be furthest from the truth; Justin was nothing if not responsible. He was single and he liked women. Things could be much worse. And speaking of women, he nibbled gently on the sweet nectar that he had before him as his conquest moaned loudly. Justin loved when they spoke the sounds of ecstasy in his direction.

Unfolding the juicy present that lay before him gave him a feeling of joy, like kids feel when they open presents; they are both excited and hopeful. Justin was excited to be traveling the canals of sexual ecstasy with one of the most beautiful women he had ever seen. He was hopeful that he could survive another round with the feisty Monica. She has held him captive for the last three days, giving him a run for his money. Justin continued to please her beyond measure, enjoying every moment of the way she was pulling in his curly locks and screaming his name. "Right there Justin...don't stop. Yes! Yes! Yes!"

He liked to swim in her ocean but before she could reach her peak, he climbed her body and entered her palace once again. In this moment, Justin turned from gentle giant to ravenous beast, pounding into Monica with abandon. Her walls collapsed around his girth, holding him captive as he dug deeper and deeper.

"That's it, baby, take this dick." He flipped her on her stomach and entered her from the back as Monica threw the roundest ass he had ever seen back at him, panting and still screaming his name.

She was about to explode, especially when Justin declared, "I'm cumming, baby...urrgghhh, ohh shit yeah!" They both reached their peak at the same time, collapsing on the bed together. Monica's body continued to enjoy silent aftershocks as she relished having *Thee Justin Brent* still nestled inside of her body. The ringing of the phone shattered the euphoric moment. Reluctantly, Justin reached for the phone.

"Yeah." His tone let the caller know he was not happy being disturbed.

It was Devlin, his campaign manager and best friend; he laughed a little as he said, "Put it back in your pants, playboy. Your little sexual hiatus with the bimbo of the week is over. I need you on deck, pronto." Devlin hung up the phone before Justin could protest.

Shaking his head and smiling at his friend's antics, Justin hung up the phone and stood to his full 6'3", stretching himself to another foot and a half as he said, "I got to go, Monica. It has definitely been a fun couple of days though." He looked over at the beauty in his bed and thought, *too bad the brains didn't come with the beauty, because she was killer in the sack.*

Monica was wearing a look of disappointment on her face as she said, "Can I come with you?"

Justin didn't even answer that ridiculous question as he headed for the power jets of his shower, hoping she would be gone when he came out.

CHAPTER 4

The Confrontation

There was plenty of excitement in the days following the announcement of the merger between Brent Electronics and Dublin Engineering. The media was relentless with their pursuit of a story. They continued to try and link the announcement to Justin's run for the Senate. Austin was anxious to separate his family's company business from his family's political life. Sitting behind his high-end oak desk, he was going over figures for the first project that would be headed under the newly merged company of Brent & Dublin Electrical Engineering.

Lately, he had been feeling bad; loss of appetite, nausea, and vomiting were threatening to ruin his day. Of the twins, Austin was the more laid-back; the one most likely to have a plan designed for everything he did. The timing of the announcement of the merger at his brother's fundraiser was not by accident.

He wanted to publicly put the bad blood between the Brent's and the Dublin's to bed. Austin and Justin could never get to the source of the conflict between the families and Jessica didn't seem to know either; however, she did confide in Austin that her father was dead set against her associating with the *Brent Bastards*. Coughing and shaking his head, Austin said, "I can't believe that's how he referred to us. He didn't even know us!"

He was jarred from his reflective thought by a slight commotion outside his office door. His office door opened and in walked Joshua Brent in all his self–importance, with the office assistant, Mildred, hot on his heels looking exasperated.

"Mr. Brent, I tried to stop him." Austin slowly raised his hand.

"Don't worry about it, Mildred." As he shot daggers at his father and said, "And what brings you to the building, Dad? You haven't stepped foot into this building since Uncle Barnacle died of cancer five years ago." Austin coughed and came from around his desk and attempted to give his father a hug, but Joshua had other plans.

"I don't plan on staying and might I say, you look horrible. I just needed to come and talk some sense into you," he said as he moved away from the intended embrace. Joshua never noticed the hurt look on Austin's face as he moved to the conference table in the corner and took a seat and continued to talk with a nervous look on his face.

"Austin, son; I really want you to reconsider your marriage to that girl. It's not too late to have it annulled! You don't know these people. They will suck you dry and spit you out. Once a Dublin, always a Dublin." He appeared to be out of breath as he completed his plea. The look on Austin's face was indifferent.

"Dad, why do you hate the Dublin's so much, surely it's not because they are black; please tell me that's not it? If you would just give Jessica a chance, you would find her to be a beautiful soul with the brain of a genius. She is good for me and even better for the company. Why can't you just be happy for us; for me?" Austin moved closer to his father, really wanting to know what was causing his father so much distress. He looked close to tears and this was something Austin had never witnessed before. He could tell this meant a lot to his father, but he refused to allow him to run his personal and business life.

Austin cleared his throat and said, "How does Mother feel about this?" Joshua shot up from his chair quicker than his sixty years should have allowed and giving his son a hard look, he said, "You will regret this." With that, he turned and moved quickly from the office, leaving a confused Austin in his wake.

CHAPTER 5

Needing a Break

Julia Custis-Brent was still the ravishing beauty she has always been, even at sixty years young. Every hair was in place and every curve was as tight as a thirty-year-old's. She still turned heads whenever she entered a room. Her beauty was natural, from her blonde locks to her statuesque figure. The relaxing massage she was receiving was helping with her stress level. It had been a week since the announcement and the tense atmosphere in her home was about to boil over as she thought to herself, *what does Jo want me to do about the situation? Our children are grown. Austin is in love. Telling them about the past will only cause more confusion than it's worth. And if the media gets wind of it!*

Julia didn't even want to dwell on what a political firestorm it would be. She was from a long line of Virginian landowners who were very active in Virginia and D.C. politics. Her father, Harold General Custis was a lobbyist who helped pass many of the laws enjoyed by citizens today. Her family was very proud and didn't aboard scandal. Julia was raised as a proper lady by a strong mother with strong Christian values. But what her mother, Henrietta Custis, didn't know was her daughter had a bit of a rebellious streak in her. Family pride reeled her in for the most part and Julia married well and raised two very fine young men; but there was the mishap thirty-three years ago that has plagued her life and marriage. The massage allowed her time to let her memory drift back to a time where her decisions almost caused disaster for her marriage.

The atmosphere in the Brent home was stifling. Julia's admission that she was carrying another man's child had all but destroyed the love and trust in their relationship. It had been a week since the disclosure, Joshua was sleeping in the servant's quarters; he had fired all of them. Julia was miserable. She felt a sense of shame, but strangely relief. The affair with Dirk had been going on for three years and had grown from a fling to a full-fledged love affair. There were no more tears left for her to shed, because what was done was done. She was thankful Joseph had not brought her family into the situation before they were able to talk things through themselves. Sitting in her room on the window bench, she pulled her legs underneath her chin and stared out into the white snow and thought how simple it looked. She thought about Dirk and what his response to her pregnancy was and smiled slightly.

The St. Regis on 16th Street has been her escape from the reality of life for the last three years. It was her piece of heaven, where she could close herself off from the world and live in the fantasy she and Dirk created. The St. Regis was only two blocks from The White House, but a world away from the hustle and bustle of politics. Whenever Joseph was away on business, which was very often, Julia and Dirk would spend the entire time closed-up in their 2500 square foot Presidential Suite. The suite was marvelous and had every luxury that could be dreamed of; from an enormous sitting room with two fireplaces, large windows and high ceilings that let the warmth of natural light shine through to the bedroom, which was her absolute favorite. It was a paradise with deep purple and gold colors accentuating the space, a huge king bed laced with Remigio Pratesi linens, and plush comforters and pillows. Dirk was rubbing oil on her feet after a relaxing bath they enjoyed together.

"Ummm, that feels so good, love," she cooed.

Dirk was always pampering her and making her feel special; something Julia felt was missing in her young life. "Baby, I will do anything to see that glow you have right now in this relaxed state," Dirk said with the sexy smile he only carried for her.

Julia knew the glow he was seeing was being helped by the package she was carrying. Fully relaxed now and gathering her courage, Julia said, "Honey, I have something I need to tell you." Noticing the seriousness in her voice, Dirk stopped kneading her feet, placing them on his lap and gave her his undivided attention. She loved how he always did that; made the things she had to say important to him, thinking, I really adore this man!

Dirk was now rubbing up and down her legs, waiting patiently for her to continue when she said, "Dirk, I am pregnant!" There, she had said it. It was out in the atmosphere. Julia had never been so scared to make a statement in her life.

Dirk felt his heart swell as he moved up Julia's body to plant kisses all over her face, saying, "I am so happy! I have always wanted children, Julia, you know that!" The excitement of the news was not overshadowed by the obvious; they were both married. That's how it was with Julia and Dirk, when they were together; they forgot about the outside world and just enjoyed each other.

Dirk offered Julia passion and excitement. He listened to her stories and let her cry on his shoulder. They were both stuck in marriages that were long past overdue for retirement; but both felt obligated to their spouses. And Julia knew she would have hell in her world, when it was revealed that she was in love with a black man, despite his pedigree. The snow outside was comforting, reminding Julia that life could get back to being that simple. Julia knew what she had to do to get her life back in balance; she had to end her relationship with Dirk.

The quiet of the huge mansion was eerie. For a home that was normally filled with laughter and love, it was truly a noticeable change. There were no maids or cooks and the lack of activity in the home was a cause for concern. Julia crept to the servant's quarters, determined to bring some clarity to the situation. As she stood in the dark fumbling for a light switch a match was struck, illuminating a gloomy-looking Joshua, who was sitting on a sofa chair with a bottle of vodka in arm's reach. His eyes held a look of disgust with a back drop of sadness. They stared at each other for what appeared to be an eternity before he spoke up.

"What do you want, Julia? Is there more exciting news you want to share with me?" The sarcasm in his voice could not be mistaken, but Julia refused to be deterred as she came closer and knelt at his feet.

"I want to talk this out, Joshua! I know I have hurt you and if you want a divorce, I totally understand. But I at least want us to talk about it first." The pain in his eyes was matched by the hurt in hers; Joshua hated to see her this way, but this was her doing, not his.

"Why, Julia? Why would you do this to us?" Joshua grabbed her shoulders and before he knew it, he was shaking her and crying. Julia didn't stop him, she felt she deserved it. "I am so sorry. I-I-I felt alone and like I needed to feel alive and loved, and instead of telling that to you, I allowed myself to fall for someone who offered those things to me without me having to ask for them." This was the first time she admitted it to herself; the acknowledgment of the reason for her deception caused tears to begin to leak from her eyes. Joshua jumped up from his seat and began pacing around the room.

"So this is my fault?" he hollered, pointing at Julia with a determined stare. "I didn't take care of your needs, so you found someone who would! Who is it, Julia, who is this man that is better for you?" He was yelling so loud that it sounded like his voice was reverberating off of the walls.

With her legs now pulled up to her chest and sobbing, Julia said just as loudly, "Dirk Dublin!" The moment it came from her mouth, she wished she could take it back. The look in Joshua's eyes went from anger to fury in seconds.

"Dirty ass Dirk Dublin! You are sleeping with the black bastard that you know has tried to ruin my family for years. What the fuck is wrong with you, Julia?" Joshua plopped down on the couch, shaking his head as the realization hit him at full speed.

The masseuse was finishing up the relaxing massage, causing Julia to push the unpleasant thoughts to the back burner. She still had to face Joshua when she returned to her life and she wasn't sure if their marriage could survive another struggle. She had to admit; her body was completely relaxed, but her mind was running a mile a minute. She hoped their tragic history would remain that; history.

It appears this marriage between Jessica and Austin is going to bring back all the bad memories whether I want it to or not, she thought as she made her way to the mani/pedi area of the spa.

CHAPTER 6

What a Day

Dropping the dumbbells to the floor, Justin let out a breath. Watching as Devlin finished his reps, he noticed they were attracting attention. One of their admirers was bold enough to walk over. She had the body of a goddess; breasts like huge grapefruits in her hot pink stretch gym clothes. She definitely had his attention when she said, "Hi!" Her voice was bubbly, making her sound like an air head; his kind of girl.

"My friend says you are Justin Brent, but I told her she was mistaken. She bet me twenty bucks. Am I a winner or a loser?" Justin began to look her up and down as he was joined by a heavy panting, Devlin, who loudly slapped both of his hands together and answered for Justin. "Sweetheart, you are definitely a winner."

Both men burst into laughter, but the girl said a little too happily, "So, you are not Justin Brent then! I told her, you don't look much like him anyway." Before he could answer, she turned on her heels to retrieve her money. When Justin and Devlin noticed the other girl reach in her fanny pack and hand over money, they couldn't help but burst out laughing again. They moved towards the weight bench, where they would take turns pressing in reps of ten. Justin believed in keeping his body straight and could bench three-fifty easily. The gym was a daily routine for Justin and Devlin. They spent the time not only getting their bodies in shape, but strategizing the campaign.

There were three meetings scheduled for today and a fundraising lunch with the League of Women Voters. It was six am when they made their way from the gym, ready to tackle the day's challenges. The two women were also leaving the gym. The bold one approached with a new twist in her hips and got right in Justin's space, saying, "I don't care that you are not a Brent, I would love to go out with you anyway!"

Justin decided not to correct her, but said, "Tell you what, sexy, give me your number and I might treat you to a time you will never forget!" Before he could get the last word out, she produced her name and number written in lipstick on a napkin and quickly turned to leave, putting an extra twist in her step. Justin shot a sly look towards Devlin as they both watched her leave, saying, "Dev, it's like taking candy from a baby." The laughter between the two friends was always welcomed.

*****

The fundraiser ended well with the Brent campaign moving closer towards its goal. Justin was mingling with constituents and listening to fond stories about their previous dealings with his father. While making small talk he noticed his sister-in-law, he smiled as he thought about her that way; she was at a table full of women laughing and sipping lemonade. He excused himself and moved with determination towards the lively group. When they noticed him standing there, they became even more animated. He walked around the table and greeted Jessica with a short hug and kiss on the cheek.

Looking around the table he asked, "What are you ladies up to? Is it something that I shouldn't be a party too?" His smile was so infectious that more than one woman blushed.

Jessica introduced each woman individually and explained they were part of the Maryland chapter of the League of Women Voters and are in full support of sending him to the Senate. As Justin graciously greeted each woman, expressing his thanks for them coming to the fundraiser that was 10,000 dollars a plate; one of the members slipped her number in his hand as he shook hers. She was stunning, a little older than what he normally liked, but her dark auburn hair and twin peaks for breasts were enough to grab his attention. As the other women discussed politics among themselves, she introduced herself as Sharon. Smiling a seductive smile, she told Justin she was a surgeon from Baltimore, Maryland. Justin was impressed; it had been a long time since he witnessed a woman with both beauty and brains that was available for the picking. Intrigued, he asked Sharon to join him for dinner so she could tell him all about her adventures.

Jessica watched the whole exchange with a slight grimace; she didn't know what to make of her playboy brother-in-law, thinking, *he is going to be a challenge!*

*****

Night had fallen on the District and Justin was preparing for his date with Sharon. Looking in the mirror, he admired his black on black Armani, his dreamy eyes and movie star looks. He was ready, but was she ready for him? He noticed something felt different about Sharon, she didn't appear to be like the normal beautiful bimbos he banged; he actually wanted to know what she thought. He laughed to himself as he made his way to his Maserati, thinking, *Could I have met my match?* The thought made him smile deeper, showing off the sexy dimples that made women cream.

Sharon was waiting in Minibar, an exclusive thirty-course restaurant in Penn Quarter. She, like most, heard about this pioneering tasting-menu-only eatery, but knew booking a reservation was harder than winning the lottery. She marveled at the exclusivity of the space, only seating six guests; and thought, *this guy really has some clout.* Her attention was directed to laughter coming from the front of the room, where Justin was shaking hands with Juan Andres, one of the most famous chefs today and the owner of the restaurant. She noticed Juan point in her direction and Justin began making his way over. Drop dead gorgeous was what she was, sitting there in a form-fitting Versace outfit. She had the prettiest eyes; they were a light shade of blue and were shaped like diamonds, or that's how they looked to him.

Once at the table, he greeted her with a kiss on the cheek, saying, "I hope you found this place with no problem?"

Looking around, he recognized the other four guests and gave them each a head nod. "I found this place just fine. My friends and I have always wanted to come." Turning his attention back to Sharon, he smiled his breathtaking smile and said, "Well I am glad you can share your first time with me." There was a sexual undertone to his words which caused her to blush, so he quickly changed the topic.

"So, Sharon, tell me about you. I mean, you know so much about me already!" Sharon told him how she did pre- med at Cornell, medical school at Columbia and her residency at John Hopkins. When their food arrived, she was explaining that she was a pediatric neurosurgeon. Justin was really intrigued.

He took a sip of his wine and then asked, "What is neurosurgery?" The smile in her eyes told him something deep about her; she loved what she did. Sharon explained neurosurgery involved the brain, central nervous system and spinal cord.

She spun the details of her chosen profession like a well-told novel. "It really covers all aspects of brain surgery, from pre-operative imaging to removal of tumors." There was a steady twinkle in her eye that was infectious. Justin couldn't believe this petite vixen performs brain surgery. It was all too much for him and he loved it. It had been years since a woman attracted him outside of the bedroom and the feeling was wonderful. They finished their meals talking about music, movies, and hobbies. They steered clear of politics and Justin appreciated the gesture.

The evening was filled with exciting discussion and delicious food. Justin and Sharon ended the night with a friendly kiss and promised to see each other again soon. For Justin, this was a new way to end the evening and he loved every minute of it. He wondered if he had found someone he could spend a lifetime with. That thought alone was so foreign to him, he not only thought about her beauty, but about the powerful political asset she would make to him. His father always told him how important the right woman on your arm was in the political game. He wasn't quite sure at first, but Sharon was causing him to think.

CHAPTER 7

Turn for the worst

Jessica and Austin were trying to relax at home. These were the times they lived for; shutting the world out and putting each other first. She was very concerned because Austin had been really sick lately; along with the loss of appetite and vomiting, he was losing a lot of weight. The over the counter drugs were not working and today she would insist they go to the hospital. Bringing tomato soup on a tray, she found Austin sleep in a recliner chair. A slight smile came across her face, because he had been trying unsuccessfully to rest and she decided not to disturb him. She promised herself if he wasn't feeling any better when he woke up, they were going straight to the hospital.

Stretching her tired muscles, she decided taking a nap might not be a bad idea. They had been working fourteen-hour days on the first merger project, both wanting to silence their critics; especially her father-in-law, Joseph Brent.

Shaking her head as she made her way to her bedroom, she said to herself, "That man is impossible." Over the years, she heard of the feud between the Dublin's and the Brent's, but it wasn't her father who told her about it. Lying in bed, she recalled the conversation with her mother that changed her outlook on life and sent her on a quest for the truth.

At twenty-eight years old, Jessica had accomplished many of her immediate goals in life. She was on point in her career as she worked hard to one day take over the company. Her personal life was hit or miss, but the one man that made her heart skip a beat was Austin Brent. She admired him from afar, but hoped to one day make his acquaintance. The only thing going wrong in her life was her mother's illness. She was suffering from dementia; Roberta Dublin was no longer the vibrant spirit in the Dublin household. One day, Jessica was brushing her mother's hair; this always seemed to relax her. Roberta was having problems with her short-term memory, but her long-term memory was sharp as a tack. The problem was, she thought the past was the present. It was hard for Jessica to see her mother this way; she took extra care as she tried to make her comfortable.

While stroking her mother's long graying hair, Roberta began to talk. "I always wanted a home full of children. Girls for me to spoil and boys for Dirk to raise in his own likeness." She sighed deeply; thinking about this appeared to be painful. "When the doctor told me I couldn't have children, we were devastated. I felt so helpless and inadequate. What kind of woman can't give her husband babies?" She began to cry slightly, causing Jessica to wrap her arms around her and say, "It's ok, Ma, because you had me and I turned out just fine."

Roberta slowly pulled away from her daughter and said in a shaky voice, "The day your father walked in this house with you, I was over the moon. We both wanted a baby so badly. We hoped a baby would heal the hurtful wounds that had occurred in our relationship. Dirk thought I didn't know, but I knew about his affair."

Jessica was shocked, she couldn't even speak; she knew her mother was ill, but was she trying to say that she was adopted, that she wasn't a Dublin? Roberta never noticed her daughter's reaction; she just continued talking as if it was important to get these things off her chest.

"It hurt me to know he was with her. As a black woman it hurt, as a wife it hurt, as a woman who couldn't give him children, it hurt. I *closed into myself and suffered in silence, but then he came home with you and my whole world changed, our whole world changed."*

Jessica was now standing in a corner, trying to digest what her mother said; she was looking at the wall as if the answers would magically appear. When she turned to see why her mother had suddenly stopped talking, she saw that her mother had fallen asleep; she had worn herself out telling her tale. Jessica wrapped a blanket around her and tried to contemplate what this information meant in her life, thinking, I can't believe they would keep something like this from me. Who are my parents? Where did I come from? Do I have siblings? *The questions that were running through her mind were causing her to get dizzy.*

Fresh tears escaped her eyes as she sat up in the bed, spent from remembering a very confusing time in her life. A week after sharing that information with her daughter, Roberta passed away in her sleep. Jessica was devastated; she lost the only mother she had ever known, but she also lost her chance to hear more stories from her mother about the past. Jessica could remember approaching her father with what her mother told her and him completely shutting her out.

He was obviously in pain, but he refused to answer any questions when it came to her past. Her father did not deny what her mother said, but he also did not confirm it. Months went by after her mother's death and Jessica threw herself into her work to keep her mind off the unraveling of her world. Her father retreated from the family business and society in general. They were barely speaking because he held so many answers for her and he refused to give them to her and that pissed Jessica off. But tonight, she would go see him, even cook dinner for him, and make every attempt to have a regular conversation with her father that didn't end in tears and yelling.

Jessica made it to her father's home before 6:00 pm with a bag of groceries to make him a huge, home-cooked meal. He was in the sitting room watching the news. He was so into the program he didn't even hear her come in. After putting the bags down, Jessica came in the sitting room and gave her father a kiss, surprising him

"Hey, sweetheart; I didn't even hear you come in. How have you been?" Taking a seat, she said, "I'm great, Dad, I missed you and I am about to make your favorite, roast beef, cabbage and rice." He gave her a slight smile and a head nod and returned his attention to the news.

Later, while they were eating dinner, her father asked her if she was dating. Jessica went into a long, drawn-out spiel about her work taking up most of her time and not finding any men worth dating, when her father interrupted her.

"Jess, please don't waste your life away with work, and have nothing to show for it in your personal life." There was a sadness in his eyes that tugged at her heart, so she thought she would attempt to lift his spirits.

"Well, Dad, there is this one guy who I am extremely smitten with. His name is Austin Brent and—" Before she could finish her sentence, her father was up from his seat and around the table, yelling and pointing in her face.

"You will not date a Brent is that clear?" Jessica had never seen this type of fire in her father's eyes; she was scared, but she wanted answers.

"Do you want to tell me what has you so upset, Dad? You were just saying how I should date."

Grabbing hold of a chair to help steady his balance, Dirk was still yelling "Stay away from them Brent's. They don't care about anybody

but themselves and in the end, you will get hurt beyond measure.
Now don't fight me on this, just let it be." With that, he slowly left the
room, seemingly drained of energy. A shocked Jessica sat at the table,
wondering how her nice dinner with her father had once again,
turned into a shouting match.

Jessica stretched as she rose from the bed. She concluded her much-needed nap was nowhere in sight, with her mind wandering over all her life's tragedies. That last dinner with her father was the beginning of a long period of silence between them. It would be almost a year before they saw each other again and when she did see her father, his health was not good. Standing in the picture window with tears rolling down her eyes, she thought about the call she received the following year, alerting her of her father's death. In two years' time, she lost the two most important people in her life. The emptiness she felt could not be measured. Add that with the uncertainty about her real parents and she was a wreck. A loud thump grabbed her attention, wiping her tears she ran down the hall, only to find Austin on the floor sweating profusely.

Jessica screamed as she ran to his side. "Austin, baby, can you hear me?" Feeling his head, he was cold as ice. Jessica ran to the phone and called 911. She then ran and got a warm towel and a blanket to attempt to warm him up. She was attempting to pick Austin up when her doorbell rang; it was the ambulance. They immediately went to work on Austin, starting an IV and placing him on the gurney. He was conscious, but not lucid.

On the ride to the hospital, Jessica was able to share the symptoms he had been experiencing and their plan to go see the doctor if he wasn't feeling better. In the midst of the chaos, Jessica was able to forget about her problems and concentrate on her husband. In the private waiting room Jessica was pacing back and forth. She called Justin and told him what happened and he was there with her within fifteen minutes. Justin was worried about his brother but he needed to be strong for Jessica.

"Hey, sis, come over here and sit down before you break those heels you are digging into the carpet!" His attempt at humor broke some of the tension in the room. She laughed and sat down next to her brother in law and exhaled.

"I'm glad you are here, Justin, 'cause I was going crazy. They haven't come back out and said anything to me." Shaking her head, she pulled her knees into her chest and rocked. Justin pulled her over to him and she rested her head on his shoulder and silently sobbed for what seemed like hours. The door to the room swung open and a short man in scrubs entered, making eye contact with Justin.

"Mrs. Brent?" Jessica jumped and moved quickly to the doctor, asking, "How is he, Dr. Roberts, can I see him?"

Reaching out and shaking Justin's hand as he approached, the doctor said, "With the symptoms of back pain, weight loss, poor appetite and digestive problems, we ran some tests on Mr. Brent's blood, urine and stool." The doctor had their undivided attention as he continued, "The blood test detected high levels of carcinoembryonic antigen and bile duct blockage." Noticing the confusing looks on their faces, he said, "There are more tests that need to be run, but when we normally see this in patients, it is normally pancreatic cancer cells." The quick intake of breath coming from Jessica caused him to stop talking as she said, "Are you saying Austin has cancer?"

Justin pulled her into his arms as tears began to fall from her eyes. Jessica didn't know if she was ready to accept another loss in her life. Dr. Roberts attempted to ease the tension in a difficult time by saying,

"We will keep him overnight, run some more tests, and get some fluids in Mr. Brent. You can see him now for a short time, but he has to get some rest and he is heavily medicated."

*****

Austin spent two weeks in the hospital and in that time, Justin has been a rock for Jessica. In the midst of everything Jessica had to make business decisions and deal with Austin's disrespectful father. *I swear, the next wrong thing comes out of his mouth, I plan on letting him see the real Jessica and he is not ready,* she thought as she stared off into space. Julia was much better, she was helpful with filling in time at the hospital so someone was always there and she kept Jessica abreast of any changes. Jessica came to the hospital every day after work to relieve her mother-in-law. On this day, Julia didn't leave; instead she said, "I think it's time we talked."

Jessica leaned down to give Austin a kiss, he was sleeping soundly. Taking off her coat and swinging it on the back of a chair, she turned to Julia and said, "Sure, let's talk." Jessica was trying to keep her tone neutral, but she was not planning on taking any shit from her mother-in-law. Julia has been nothing but gracious and helpful to Jessica. She has not been overtly opposed to their marriage, but Jessica couldn't help but feel like the other shoe was about to drop. Julia walked over to the window and leaned against the ledge and began.

"We have a complicated history, the Brent's and Dublin's. I hurt my husband very deeply and Dublin's remind him of that pain, so he will never sanction this marriage." Jessica started to interrupt, but Julia held up her hand, saying, "Let me get this out. I still have not worked out in my own heart how I feel about this marriage, but I won't speak against this marriage either. I would like for us all to try and be a family and let the past be the past."

Letting out a breath, Julia looked in her daughter-in-law's confused eyes. Jessica didn't quite know what to say to her. Just like her father, Julia was vague as to what the issue between the families was, and Jessica was too tired to argue the issue. She said, "My only concern is Austin's health. I can't be concerned with what the Brent's and Dublin's are arguing about. I got my own problems and you guys' history doesn't affect me and my husband's future; I love him and that should be enough." Julia smiled and gave Jessica a hard nod, saying, "Yes, that should be enough." Grabbing her coat to prepare to leave, Julia watched the love and care that Jessica gave to her son and for her, that was enough.

CHAPTER 8

Family Secrets

With everything happening in her life, Jessica just needed to relax. The only problem was her nerves were way too jumpy to relax. Austin was still in the hospital and his father insisted on spending the day with him. Jessica refused to be in his presence; instead she decided to go to her parents, house. Over the years, she shied away from spending any real time in the house she grew up in; the memories were just too great. But today she hoped to find some type of peace and much-needed security. Standing in the sitting room of her family home caused a rush of emotions to come crashing down and Jessica had to grab onto the nearest couch for support. She could almost feel her parents sitting in the room near the fireplace; her mom knitting something, while her father watched the news.

This was the one room in the house everyone converged on after their long day to just be in each other's space. This was the room where some of the happiest moments in the Dublin family were spent. She remembered sitting on the couch and debating topics from the engineering world with her father well into the night; they were happy. Sighing heavily, Jessica began to move around the room, picking up mementoes along the way and smiling. The adjoining room was her father's sanctuary; his office. Jessica and her mother never entered this holy place, but today she felt like going through his things, if for nothing more than to get her mind off her own problems.

The office was immaculate. Jessica still had the house serviced weekly by a maid and gardener. The room smelled of pine and oak cleaner. There was a huge Royal Oak desk near the floor to ceiling window. There were papers on the top of the desk that had now been sitting for three years. Shaking her head, Jessica began to read through them, they were invitations to fundraisers, household bills, and insignificant mailings. At the reading of her father's will, she was given a set of keys and told they were to his desk and his home safe and safe deposit box. Jessica never found the energy or time to go through these things before, but today she would move forward despite her reservations; *it has been long enough*, she thought. Using her key, she opened the desk and riffled through it; there were the usual tidbits one would expect in a desk. The last drawer of the desk contained a Barska top opening desk safe. She fumbled with the keys until she found the one that opened the safe. Inside was money, an extra copy of his will and an envelope with her name on it.

For a long while, she just looked at the contents of the safe. An uneasy feeling came over her; it was like removing things from this safe was internally acknowledging her parents were never coming back. She knew they were not, but staying away from the house and not going through her father's things kept the reality at bay. Deciding now was the time, Jessica slowly pulled the envelope out, holding it in her hand a bit longer before she ripped it open; as he eyed the contents, she silently cursed herself for waiting so long to go through her father's things. Inside was a bank statement from an account in the Grand Cayman Islands that was in her father's name, but listed her as the co-owner.

Three years ago, the balance in the account was a little over three million dollars. Jessica just stared at the paper in awe; she couldn't believe she had that type of money. She didn't understand why this money wasn't covered in the will, which already left her a significant amount of money and property. Still holding onto the statement that

solidified she was rich; Jessica pulled more papers out of the envelope.
There was a letter addressed to her.

My lil Jess,

*If you are reading this, than that means your old man has lost the
great fight; I'm sorry, darling. I hate we have both left you by yourself,
but I hope we have equipped you with the skills and assets to
continue on without us. I know you have now seen you are a very
wealthy lady. I didn't include this money in the will, because it is
untraceable. That is why it is in a Cayman account; keep your money
over there safe from government scrutiny and the grasp of anyone
whom you might marry in the future. I want you to know that your
mother and I love you so much and I know you have a lot of
questions that I refused to answer in life, but I will now answer in
death. I am not proud to say that I fell in love with another woman
while I was married to your mother. I loved this woman with
everything that was in me. At the same time, I was very much in love
with your mother. My heart was split in two separate directions, but I
would have never left Roberta.*

*What your mother told you was true, she could not have children,
so you are not her biological daughter, but you were the light that
brightened her heart every day; I'm sure you know this. I never
wanted to hurt Roberta, but after she realized she couldn't have
children, she entered a level of depression that no matter what I did, I
couldn't help her overcome it. So, I sought out affection in other
places, namely Julia Brent. At the end of the day, Julia got pregnant by
me and Joshua made her get rid of our baby. She knew how much I
wanted a baby, but she didn't care; it was more important to save her
already damaged marriage. So, you can see why I want you to steer
clear of that family. They don't care about anyone but themselves. I*

want you to live a happy and healthy life. Find a nice young man and settle down and get married. But please know your parents loved you with everything they had in them and nothing else matters. I love you, my lil Jess.

Your Father

Finishing up the letter, Jessica felt more confused than when she was before. She was feeling like the Brent's and Dublin's were keeping things about her life from her that she deserved to know. Tears rolled down her face as she thought about her mother telling her the story about her father coming home with a baby. Where did that baby come from? Who were her parents? At thirty-three, some people could probably let this go, the millions of dollars are a huge incentive, but Jessica was tired of everyone else having a say-so over her life. She was gonna start fucking with their lives and see how they liked that. Stuffing the papers in her purse, Jessica decided she had seen enough. Her mind was spinning a mile a minute and she truly had some decisions to make. Some people were going to suffer if she didn't get some answers.

CHAPTER 9

That Political Life

The media got wind of Austin's medical problems and were relentless in their attempt to make it a top issue in Justin's run for the Senate. At every moment they wanted to know if there was any way Justin's medical condition should be looked at more closely, since he is Austin's twin. Devlin gave a blanket statement, attesting to Justin's perfect health and attempted to steer the topic to the Senate race. Devlin had Justin making speeches about his business sense with his background from Brent Electric, and his political family history and the integrity he gained from growing up in such an environment.

During a strategy meeting, Justin got a text from Sharon; he smiled as he read her witty line of the day. They have been dating two to three times a week since that first date. Justin could hardly believe he was feeling one woman this much. He didn't know if he turned in his playa card as Devlin suggested, but he knew he was very interested in her. The one thing that surprised him the most was they had not had sex yet. They were so busy enjoying each other's company that the sex talk hadn't even surfaced. That alone makes her special, because usually the bedroom is Justin's only agenda when it comes to women. Sharon actually is making him look at the situation differently.

Devlin was watching his boss laugh at his cell phone and he knew it had to be Sharon. He thought she was good for Justin's image, she was sexy as hell, a neurosurgeon and able to keep the over-sexed Justin at bay. Shaking his head and smiling, Devlin said to himself, *she might be a keeper.* Writing something on a pad, he passed a note to his assistant that read, *Vet Sharon Rector from Baltimore, Maryland,*

John Hopkins Hospital. Justin paid Devlin to think ahead and right now he was thinking about finding out more about this amazing woman before the media got wind of her.

Justin was texting back and wearing a silly grin, when the other staff members walked in the room. The meeting started and Devlin laid out some specific game plans and timelines. Justin spoke to his staff as he liked to do; there was his social media staff who kept him relevant in cyberspace. His Facebook handle is JustinBrent4Senate, his Twitter is JBrentSenate, and the Instagram is SenateJBrent. Each account was run by a different member of the media team and they were invaluable to the election process.

At the close of the meeting, everyone was more energized and ready to hit the pavement running. Justin stayed back with Devlin for their private meeting. This is where the real strategizing started. Devlin leaned back in his chair and stretched his arms above his head, saying, "How is Austin?"

Justin was getting a bottled water out of the fridge as he said, "The test has not confirmed the diagnosis. They are just keeping him a couple of more days to get his fluid levels back up to par, because he was so severely dehydrated." Moving back to the table, Justin had a somber look on his face.

"I just can't believe he is sick. Our Uncle Barnacle had pancreatic cancer, but it wasn't diagnosed until later in life, or he didn't let us know about it, but he did always appear to be sick. I just don't want that for Austin."

Devlin had known the twins for years and was fond of them both, so he knew exactly how Justin was feeling.

"Well, I have cleared your schedule. Take some time and go visit your brother. Julia has already called and insisted." That brought a smile to both of their faces. Leave it to his mother to throw her weight around when it came to her boys.

"Alright, I'm gonna go over there now. Appreciate your concern." Before he could leave, he received another text from Sharon that read, *I think it's time that you and I got to know each other better *wink* meet me at the St. Regis at 8 pm penthouse suite.*

Despite his inner despair, there was a smile on his face that could light up a dark room. Devlin noticed and shaking his head, said, "Must be an invite from Sharon!" Justin turned to face his dear friend who knew him so well and said, "Yep, inviting me to the St. Regis, so you know what that means."

Devlin did know what that meant. He just wondered would Sharon survive or would she become like Justin's other conquests, who he would throw away like yesterday's trash after he slept with them; only time would tell.

*****

Austin was awake when Justin made his way into his room. He was sitting up, watching the business news.

"Hey, bro, why you watching that depressing stuff?" Austin tried to laugh at his silly brother, but started coughing uncontrollably. Justin immediately got him water to sip as he watched helplessly as his other half went through the most painful time in his life.

"Aus, I hate seeing you like this, man. I don't know anyone I love more than you and you're scaring me, man." The brothers stared at each other, both silently knowing their time together was limited.

"Don't be scared, bro! I'm not. I am sad though. I got a wonderful wife who I am depriving of what she wants most in this life and that's family. Dad is treating her like a pariah for some shit between him and her dad that none of us knows about or understands, and I feel like I should be able to make it better for her." The sadness in his voice could not be missed.

Justin wanted to assure his brother Jessica was alright, but he didn't know because he hadn't seen her in a couple of days, so he asked, "Where is Jessica anyway?"

Austin got a far-off look on his face and said, "She was here earlier, but Dad was here as well so she didn't stay long. But I could tell something was different with her, I just couldn't put my finger on it." Justin felt himself getting angry that his father insisted on having his way in this instance. He has always been that way, and Justin made a note to himself to speak with him about it.

He grabbed his brother's hand and said, "Tomorrow, I will check on Jessica. And I am definitely going to have a talk with Dad; he has got to let old shit go." The brothers shake hands and spend time talking about football.

Austin was an Eagles fan and Justin was a Redskins fan, so the conversation was getting so heated, they didn't even notice Julia enter the room. She just leaned up against the wall and watched her boys argue about football like they did back when they were young. She bottled that feeling up inside of her heart and never wanted to let it go. The debate was raging on about who would take the Super Bowl and each brother was insistent their team would be playing. Julia had to laugh out loud at that.

"Now you boys know good and well the Redskins and the Eagles will not have any post-season play, haaaaaaaaaa." The Brent's all joined in for some much-needed laughter as they continued with their debate together.

CHAPTER 10

St. Regis

Justin hadn't had that much fun with his family in a long time; it was just the therapy they needed. Austin was fast asleep when he left. His mother decided she would sit with him through the night. She had a look of pain in her eyes Justin wished he could take away. He said a silent prayer for his family as he made his way towards the parking lot. There was nothing he wanted more than to see his family being able to have more moments like tonight.

With those thoughts weighing heavy on his mind, Justin made his way home to get ready for his date with Sharon. Just thinking about tasting her was making his male member stand at attention. That could also be because he hadn't had sex since he started dating her. Whatever the cause, one thing for sure was every time he thought about her, he was happy they have been spending so much time together. Smiling to himself, he thought, *this commitment stuff isn't that bad, I might try it.* Smiling at his silliness, he grabbed his car keys and made his way towards the Regis.

The night air was pleasant as Justin pulled his drop-top Jaguar up to the valet. He always liked the elegance of the St. Regis; it gave off a regal air with a contemporary feel. Once he entered the lobby, the gigantic chandeliers sparkled throughout the foyer. There was no way you wouldn't be impressed with the opulence. Justin made his way to the gold-plated elevators, thinking, *it appears we have the same taste, that's a good thing.*

The ride to the penthouse seemed longer than it was; the classical music of Bach was playing, adding to the feel of sophistication of the ride. The doors opened to the penthouse foyer and he was treated to the luxury of rich burgundy and gold furnishings. There was elegant finishing details and artwork throughout the corridor. Justin moved towards the architecturally designed double door and tapped lightly. He couldn't believe he was a little nervous about the step he was about to take with Sharon. When the door opened, he was at a loss for words; he couldn't get the words out of his mouth, but he couldn't stop looking at the butt-naked beauty before him either. The areola of her breasts was so luscious; Justin was literally salivating in the doorway. He had never noticed how curvaceous she was; her hips screamed to be licked from one side to the other.

Her perfectly manicured toes glistened with a candy apple red topping and the thickness of her thighs was any man's dream play-land. Standing there taking her all in was causing his manhood to stand at attention, like a well-trained soldier ready to report for duty. And he was definitely ready to report. When he was finally able to steal his eyes away from her well-endowed assets and catch his breath, he looked her in her lust-filled eyes that were only matched by his own and said, "Jessica, what are you doing here?"

A RACE FOR CHASE
"CINCINNATI LOVE STORY"
Author Quintessa Turner

July 2005, is a year that I would never forget. It was a hot sunny day, so I had on some short booty shorts, white tank top, thong sandals and my hair was in a fresh doobie wrap. I was walking down Glenwood Avenue, headed to my apartment. I glanced towards the street, because out of nowhere a blue 1999 Dodge Plymouth pulled up in the middle of the street beside me.

This milk chocolate guy, rolled down his window and yelled, "What's up, shorty?" I kept walking, pretending that I didn't hear him. I always thought it was very disrespectful to approach a female like that. He then repeated himself.

"What's up, shorty? I know you hear me, with them little bitty ass shorts on." I stopped and looked at him with an attitude.

"Look nicca, my name is not shorty. That's not how you approach me."

"Then what is your name?"

"What do you want to know for?" I asked.

"Maybe I like what I see."

"Nicca, you only see what's on the outside; you don't really know what you like"

"Look, girl, are we going to keep going back and forth, or should I keep it moving?" He asked, putting his car in park in the middle of the street and jumping out. The guy that was on the passenger side was laughing at him as he approached me. Before I could say anything, he grabbed my phone and began dialing numbers. Apparently, he was calling his own cell phone because it started ringing. The whole time he had my phone, my mouth was just hanging open in shock. It's crazy because at any other time, I would have smacked someone for doing something like that. Once my number appeared across his phone, he hung up.

He then programmed his name to the number in my phone and then gave me my phone back. When I looked down, the number was saved under "Chase". He completely caught me off guard.

"So, Ms. Lady not Shorty, what should I save your number under?" he questioned, laughing and smiling at the same time. "London," I told him in a shocked tone. His smile had my insides dancing. I had never had a guy make me feel that way.

"Look, I am going to call you later when I am finish working. Make sure you answer, I don't want to have to come find you, because I don't give up easy when I see something that I want," he said, running back to his car that was now holding up traffic.

I laughed and continued walking towards my apartment. When I approached my apartment building, there was this big black van with tinted windows sitting in the driveway. The doors were open and a lot of guys were sitting inside of it.

I glanced over and one of the guys looked familiar. They were staring at me and I heard someone say, "Come here, London." When I took a second look, it was this guy named Dan. He and his crew were known for kidnapping people. They called themselves the Grimy Network. I ran as fast as I could without stopping, into my apartment building all the way to my apartment on the third floor. I was out of breath, but I didn't feel safe until I got to my door.

Soon as I reached my door there was a note attached, asking if I wanted my apartment exterminated for roaches. I was pissed, opening my door. I had not even been living in this apartment for two months and I had roaches. Soon as I walked in the door, sure enough, fucking roaches were having a ball in the middle of the kitchen floor. The messed-up part about it is, I bleach my apartment down every day, but they just keep coming; I just let they ass be. I was so exhausted from the humidity and running up the steps, I just stripped down to my panties and bra and lay in my bed. Before you knew it, I dozed off and the TV was watching me.

It felt like I had just closed my eyes when I was awakened by the sound of my phone ringing. Chase's name appeared across the screen. I didn't answer until the fourth ring.

"Hello," I said in a tired, dry tone.

"What's up, London?"

"Who is this?" I asked, pretending I didn't know who he was.

"Come on now, girl, you seen my name pop across your phone."

"Actually, I picked up the phone without even looking at the number," I lied. "Well, it's Chase, can you come outside?"

"For what? I don't even know you," I said, giving him attitude.

"I just want you to ride with me and talk. I'm outside your building now."

"Nicca, how do you know where I live?"

"Girl, just come out," he retorted, sounding like a girl.

I laughed at him, but as bad I wanted to play hard to get; I gave in. "Give me a few minutes."

"Okay! Don't take all day; you know these niccas over here ain't right," he said, hanging up the phone.

I jumped up, brushed my teeth and put on some jeans, a V-neck tee shirt and some sandals. I grabbed my purse and keys on the way out the door. Chase was sitting in front of the building, and this time he was in a different car. As I approached the car, I could smell marijuana coming from the cracked window. I don't smoke, but I loved the smell. When I opened the car door, he was smiling from ear to ear, looking at me and ending a phone call at the same time.

My insides started dancing just like they did earlier. His cologne was intoxicating; if I was a hoe, I could have jumped on top of him right in front of my building and fucked the shit out of him. I don't know why, but he looked different now that I could look directly in his face. He was milk chocolate, with wavy hair, kind of chubby and his teeth were as white as a fresh white tee out the pack.

I guess I was staring at him a little too hard, because his ass was snapping his fingers in my face laughing, which made me start laughing. We rode around through Clifton, Downtown, and Evanston. His phone was ringing nonstop, but it never appeared to be a female that he was fucking with; he always answered with, "What's up, sis or bruh?" I never understood that language.

"London, we've been riding around for a little minute, are you hungry? Do you want to go to the movies or something?"

"I'm cool; I'm just really enjoying this time with you," I lied. I was hungry as fuck. Truth be told, I don't like eating around guys that I don't know.

"Well, I'm hungry. I know this little chicken spot in Roselawn that has some bomb ass chicken. The best in the city to be exact," he said with confidence.

"The spot up by Club Celebrities?" I asked.

"Yeah, that's it."

The rest of the ride was silent, with nothing but the sound of the music playing, until we got to the restaurant. All I could think about was, *what have I gotten myself into with this guy?* I'm young as hell, riding around with this grown ass man; he has to be 25 or older. He doesn't look like it, but the way he talks, he has the mind of someone who is older.

When we approached the restaurant, he parked and then walked around and opened my door. My insides danced again. He just keeps doing things to me without even touching me. Pretty soon, he is going to notice a wet spot on my jeans. Before he shut the door, I noticed he reached in the glove department and grabbed what appeared to be a gun and placed it on the right inside of his jeans. A lump formed inside of my throat. Hell naw, now it feels like I am dancing with the devil. This nigga got me riding around with guns and weed.

I remember my older brother telling me to always watch my surroundings in public. How cautious Chase's actions, being cautious walking through the parking lot, told me he stood by that as well. I felt safe with him, but still scared. Soon as we walked into the restaurant, the guys that were standing around waiting on their food shook his hand and they did a little small talk. I heard one of the guys say, "What's up, Meek?" I looked twice at him and made a mental note to ask him about this "Meek" character. The workers behind the counter had started making his food before he even told them his order. I guess he was a real regular, VIP-style. He had them add on a fry and some chicken tenders for me, although I didn't plan on eating it until I got home. Something still wasn't sitting right with me, because as I played out the day and put everything together, I came right back to the point that I don't even know this guy.

My brother told me to always find out as much as you can when it comes to niccas, because you don't know what type of work they do or who they are beefing with. I did none of that. I guess he could see that my mood had changed when we got back in the car, because we were driving in silence. Out of nowhere, blue lights appeared behind us. My street instincts kicked in once again.

I quickly asked him, "Do you have any drugs in the car?" as he pulled over. He said, "Yeah, only a small bag of marijuana." I unzipped my pants and stuffed the small bag up in my vagina, I left my pants unzipped and pretended that my stomach hurt. He had a secret compartment in the car where he stashed his gun. I looked in my rear mirror and saw two police cars pull up behind us. All I could do is look at him and look away. *This nicca must have hella warrants; why else would they come this deep to pull him over?*

Two officers approached the car on each side. Chased rolled down the window without hesitation. "Excuse me, sir, can I see your license and insurance?" the officer asked him.

Chase kept one hand on the steering wheel and grabbed his license and insurance card from the cup holder with the other hand. He quickly gave it to the officer that was on his side. Then the officer walked back to his car. The other officer that was on my side of the window was looking all in the car, through the window. He then asked me to step out of the car. I did as I was told, but still pretended my stomach was hurting. I got out the car bent over holding my stomach. He asked, "Are you ok? Why are your pants unzipped?"

"I just found out that I'm pregnant and my stomach was hurting really bad." He fell for it, but I thought he was going to call a lady officer to come search me. From what I know, male police officers are not allowed to search women. To my surprise he didn't, he just walked back up to the car and had Chase get out of the car. "Sir, do you know why I pulled you over?" the officer asked Chase.

"No sir, but you can tell me," Chase responded back.

"For one, your tint is too dark; it's over the legal limit and every time you continue to drive with this dark tint, you will get pulled over."

"Wow, I didn't know that, sir; I've had this can for a couple months and this is the first time that I have heard such a thing."

"You know I could take you to jail right now for being a smart ass and possession of marijuana."

"With all due respect, Officer; I don't have no marijuana. I had some, but it's gone; I smoked it. And I'm just being honest. You can search the car if you would like."

I laughed so hard in my head, because Chase was being a real smart ass but in a respectful way. Before the officer could respond, the other officer approached Chase, but called him by his government name, I'm guessing.

"Meeks Chase Miller, I just knew I had something on you, when I ran you through the system but that part is clean. My partner and I are going to search the car and if we don't find anything, we will let you and the young lady go." We stood off to the side in the grass and I prayed that they didn't find that compartment that he had the gun in. I stared in the car and the whole time I was watching them, I could feel Chase looking at me with a smirk. Ten minutes later, they came back over to us and handed Chase back his license and insurance card.

"Y'all are free to go. But, if we ever pull you over again and smell marijuana, we will arrest you for probable cause, even if we didn't find anything." He just gave them the head nod and we got in the car and pulled off.

I immediately demanded of him, "Take me home." He did as I asked and the ride was silent once again. When we approached my building, it was one o'clock in the morning and no one was out. Soon as he put the car in park, I gripped the door handle and tried to jump out, but he locked the doors so I couldn't get out. I just sat back in the seat.

"What you mad for, London?" he asked.

"It's so much shit, Chase; I mean Meeks, where the fuck should I start?"

He laughed like everything was cool and nothing I said was serious. "You know you real sexy when you're mad, London." He laughed again. "Start wherever you want, baby, I got time."

"So, why did you tell me your name was Chase and not Meeks? Who gives out their middle name?" I asked.

"Well, I gave you the name Chase, because my name holds weight out here and it don't take a rocket scientist to know the type of shit I do. I'm not the average, I was going to eventually tell you, but shit you found out sooner than expected. It's a lot of shit that I'm not proud of behind the name Meeks. I've had niccas send pretty bitches at me just to try and rock me to sleep.

I be damn if I let a bitch be my downfall. I'm trying to turn over a new leaf. So what now?"

"What do you mean so what now, Chase, I mean Meeks? I don't really know what to call you. Why the fuck would I try to get you for some niccas? Nicca, you stopped me and forced your number in my phone."

"No disrespect, baby, but the quickest way to get caught slipping is women and you caught my attention."

I was so tired of going back and forth with him. I don't what the fuck to call this nicca. I don't know if I'm down for anything that he has attached to him. I seem to always attract these niccas with baggage. *I just stuffed some weed in my pussy for this nigga and he's coming at me like I am a jack bitch?* I sat in silence, thinking.

Man, I don't even know if I really want to show this girl my other side since I already told her a little bit about me already or do I really turn over a new leaf and she only know Chase. I know I can't tell her too much because I still don't even really know her. But I can say she know how to cover for a nigga I can give her that. Shit could have gone all the way left when we got pulled over but she held shit down. Chase thought to his self as he stared out the window.

"Shit could have gone all the way left when we got pulled over, but you held shit down. You covered for a nicca, 'preciate it. So, where do we go from here?" Chase said, breaking the silence.

"I really don't even know," I responded back as I dug in my pants and pulled the weed out my vagina.

"Do you have an extra bag to dump this in? I don't want to give it back to you like this."

"Naw, you straight, I'll take it back just like that; I'm sure your shit doesn't stank," he answered, laughing.

"I really hope that we can move forward or start over. I really wanna show you who Chase is. Chase can show you a good time and honest to God, you would be the first female to grow with Chase. I don't want you to know Meeks because there is nothing good behind him but beef, bitches, and bullshit. So what's up?" he said, while staring directly in my face.

"This is all a bit much; I'll call you when I cool off." I handed him the bag of marijuana, while hitting the unlock button and hopping out the car.

Chase rolled down the window when he saw about to open the door to my apartment building. "Aye, London, don't let too much thinking make you miss out on something good."

All I did was look back and then disappeared into the building.

Man, this girl is going to be a piece of work. Chase thought to himself as he rode away. The sun was coming up so that meant he had to go shower and get his day started. "I can't believe I just experienced all this nonsense. How do I go from meeting a guy I think is nice, to him possibly being a damn nightmare! I have to think all this over and talk to my brother, Chris," I said, talking to myself. The rest of the morning for me just consist of taking a hot bath, eating, and finally getting some sleep. Well, at least I thought I was getting some sleep until I heard a bang at the door. Jumping up and grabbing my robe, I went to answer the door.

"Who is it?"

"Chris. London, open the door; I have to shit."

As I opened the door, Chris rushed past her and went straight to the bathroom. "Boy, why you always pick my house to come shit at? Your crib is less than fifteen minutes away."

"Exactly fifteen minutes away and I was riding right past your house. Besides, I haven't heard from you in a couple days; what's going on? I usually would have gotten a call from you. You haven't called and checked ah nicca's pulse or nothing," Chris said while he was sitting on the toilet.

I was hesitant to even break the news to him, but one thing for sure and two for certain I never kept any secrets from him. We were like the white and yoke inside of an egg. I stood outside the bathroom door with her back up against the wall, silent.

"I know you standing outside the door, London; you better start talking before I beat your ass for hiding some shit from me," Chris said in a demanding tone. I knew he meant what he said when he gave me that tone.

"Well, I met this guy earlier yesterday; he pushed down on some boss shit. He seemed real cool. To make a long story short, he picked me up later that night and I rode around with him. He told me his name was Chase, but when we were out, I heard niccas we ran into at this restaurant in Roselawn, call him by a whole other name."

"Girl, you tripping, nicca get called anything. So, what next?" he chimed in. "We ended up getting pulled over, he had weed in the car and I stuffed it like Gina said she did when y'all got pulled over, but it was way less than what she had. The cops searched the car didn't find anything, but when one of the cops gave him back his license and insurance card, they called him by the name that he had given me and the name that I heard the niccas at the restaurant call him. So, I was pissed and made him bring me home. He told me he didn't tell me the other name, because he didn't wanna involve me with the beef, bullshit, and bitches. He said he didn't have beef with no one, but basically being the type of nigga he is brings that drama. He said he really wanted to try and make some things work with me and turn over a new leaf. I don't know though."

Chris was quiet; all I heard was the, the toilet flush and the sink water turn off. When he opened the bathroom door, he was drying his hands. "So what's this nicca's name? You done said everything but this nicca's name."

"Meeks is what the niccas called him, but Chase is the name he gave me."

"Meeks? I heard about him; for the most part I've heard good things. He getting to it and he takes good care of his peoples. But be careful, I actually just heard some niccas up the way that fuck with my people say he was they next target. So, if you really trying to fuck with dude, you need to take up all his time and keep him out the way. I'll keep my ear to the streets since you rocking with dude. I definitely ain't about to let nothing happen to you. I'll make a couple calls, just do what I said."

I felt a lump form in my throat. Just what I thought; I walked into some bullshit. But since I got the word, I feel I should still pass the information that my brother just related to me to Chase.

"Ok, Chris; I'll do that."

Chris grabbed a water out of the fridge and laid down on the couch. I went back to bed and tried to get some sleep again.

Chase didn't know if he was coming or going, the more he tried to clean his hands with the streets the more shit seem to come his way. Turning over a new leaf was more difficult than he thought. He tried to wash up all his money that was from drug money by opening up a few businesses. He wanted to move out of Cincinnati for good once the business were up and running. He also wanted London to be apart of that new transaction. Yes, he just met her but, the move she pulled when they got pulled over by the police showed how real she was from jump. He did his homework on her an word is she is a good girl, nobody had nothing bad to say about her.

He wanted to wait for her to call him because he has not never been the type to chase a female once she had an attitude, they always find their way back to him. London had a hold on him though so... He called her but her phone rung and went to the voicemail. He shot her a text saying he was just checking on her and if she wanted to talk call him.

I saw Chase had called and texted me about an hour ago, so I called him back. "Hello, Chase, I saw that you called me, and I got your text."

"What's up, London?"

"I need to see you, so we can talk. Are you able to come get me?"

"I can be there within an hour. Is everything ok with you?"

"Yes, I am fine; I just need to talk to you face-to-face."

"Ok, see you in a few." Chase was happy London called but she had him a little concerned usually when females want to talk to him in person it's always bullshit. Just as he'd spoken he arrived at my house a little less than an hour. I was already standing outside dressed in a black maxi dress and some sandals. Soon as his car came to a stop, I hopped in.

"What's up, London?"

"Well, I got some disturbing news!"

"About what?"

"You! I was talking to my brother about last night and mentioned your name, and he said he heard from his peoples up the way that some niccas from Columbus was plotting on you!"

"Word? Who is your brother?"

"Chris."

"Lil Chris from Evanston?"

"Yeah, why; you know him?"

"Not on a personal level, but I heard he get to it and he's a good guy."

"That's strange, because he said the same thing about you! He also said he will take care of that Columbus situation on behalf of me fucking with you."

"Word, that's some real G shit."

"I also wanna apologize for the way I overreacted and to let you know I'm willing to give Chase a chance."

"Damn girl, you got a nicca blushing and shit," Chase said, laughing and smiling ear to ear.

"Let's get away from all this madness, so I can really get to know Chase; let the streets die down."

"It's funny you said that, because I was just saying I needed to get away. We can leave right now. You can buy clothes and shit when we get to where we are going."

"I'm down," I said, kissing Chase on the cheeks. I'm excited and relieved that I got to tell him everything and how I felt. Maybe things will work out between the two of us. We drove down 71 to75 South, headed to Atlanta, Georgia. On the drive down, Chris called me.

"Aye, London, tell Meeks he good and everything's taken care of."

Just like that, Chris kept his word and didn't waste no time handling business. One thing he didn't play about is his sister. He knew that by me fucking with Meeks aka Chase, I would be with him a lot outside, and he just didn't want things to go wrong while I was with him.

****

They say you can meet someone and fall in love at first sight, and my insides danced when Chase smiled at me. So, Racing for Chase was definitely worth it.

THE TRIANGLE
Author Jo Dee

My name is Kwaku which means "born on Wednesday" in Ghana. My friends call me Kae and tonight 1 stopped believing in love. Not that 1 was much of a believer to begin with. Some might think of me as a bit of a player but tonight everything changed.

"1 think you made a mistake," 1 told my traveling companion.

"Look closer Kwaku... did 1," she replied.

1 peered into the bedroom window of this strange home and found a nightmare waiting for my eyes to focus on. Recognition lived in my vision. Shock flowed through my veins and hatred pumped through my heart. 1 saw two familiar tattooed feet spread wide, saw my lover, saw the woman 1 wanted to marry in ecstasy without me being a part of the ugly that made up her cum face. 1 turned and ran with my traveling companion on my heels; the individual who had brought me to this nightmare, one with ulterior motives herself. She caught up to me, turned me toward her, made me face her.

"I'm sorry Kwaku. 1 truly am." 1 looked at her through wet eyes, shook my head, tried to figure out the how and the why of things. My mind instantly went back to the beginning. It all started a few months ago... 1 was just getting out of a very superficial relationship with a woman that 1 knew wasn't wifey material, hell she wasn't even Netflix and chill material but the roll of her hips and the suction of her lips could bring any man to his knees.

Damn! 1 had met her while she was sitting at the city bus-stop and 1 pulled up and kicked some lines to her. The chick was a looker with hazel eyes, light brown skin and curves for days. Her skin was as full of ink as her vocabulary was as lacking in words. To put it mildly, she was basic but "fuckable" and "fuckable" was all I was after.

We kicked it for about three months until her main man got out of jail on some bullshit he had gotten himself into and she went scurrying back to the drug dealer life. Hood rat that she was, I didn't blame her. Anyway, a drought ensued after that and so I decided to give online dating a shot once more.

I had used the web once before for a time and found that most of the women were middle-of-the-road chicks with some huge flaw always hidden at first but surfaced at a later date. The web was full of clingy chicks, crazy chicks, chicks to loose with the golden goose, health nut chicks and last but definitely not least were the holier than thou chicks spouting God this and Jesus that with their half naked profile pictures on full display. I definitely didn't want to use those sites again. A friend had told me to try this site called Topdimes.com.

He had found the love of his life there so I said to myself...why not me. The site was full of professional eye candy and I couldn't wait to dive into the flesh that awaited me there. Before putting up a profile of my own, I decided to browse the site and see what sort of women they had to offer. Right away, I noticed there was one requirement prevalent in every profile that I had skimmed through. It was same as when I had used other sites before. A simple moniker that stood out to me for some odd reason now. It didn't in the past, but it did now.

"No pic...no reply" was proudly displayed somewhere in every profile I had come across. I guess image is everything, even for professional women, who one would think had evolved pass (looks first everything else second) mentality. But there it was, physical attraction seemed to be the first trait on everyone's list. It gave me cause to pause. Believe me, I could be as shallow as the next person but for some reason I was expecting something different from these type of women. I don't know why. I knew I was an attractive man. I had always been confident in my 6'3 two hundred and fifteen pound frame. My father was a black American and my mother hailed from the motherland. She was Ghana which meant I was Ghana. I had inherited the best of both traits from both of my chromosome donors. But while I was appealing to the eyes and appreciated ladies who were as well, I now found myself craving a woman with substance. A better version of me, someone who appreciated my mind as well as the thickness I had hanging that made her moan. So the "no pic" thing distracted me briefly.

After browsing the harem of potential "Miss Rights", I decided to make a profile myself. I figured I'd let some come to me instead of me doing all of the chasing. I loved aggressive women anyway and wasn't intimidated like some men were. Shiid, bring on miss independent. Hell, I figured I needed someone with some spunk to handle all of this chocolate anyway. I debated briefly about using a pic myself and just allowing my words to describe me and pique their interest.

I was a talented communicator born with the gift of gab. In the end, I decided on just one. After about an hour at it, I was satisfied with what I had come up with and proceeded to log out and close everything down for the night when...ping. I had a new message that quickly. My first response to a profile I had just finished five minutes ago. I opened up the message.

It read as follows: *Hi there...I came across your profile and I must admit you have piqued my curiosity which is a hard feat to accomplish. I would welcome the opportunity to get to know you better. If I am aligned with what you are searching for, I hope to hear from you soon. Until we connect.*

Simone

I read her note over and over, smiled with each reading. I enjoyed her choice of words, knew her to be some type of writer with the way she formed her sentences and conveyed her thoughts. I was intrigued already! I didn't want to jump at the first bite but just that small paragraph of words had gotten me hooked. I wanted to learn more about this woman so just like the hypocrite that I am, I immediately went to her page to see what this lady looked like.

I stared at the image that looked back at me. Simone L Davis she had her middle initial posted with her name. Cute. Simone was a rich dark brown skin beauty. Judging by her pic, her diet was exceptional because her skin was flawless. She had dark piercing eyes, a small symmetric nose accompanied by some of the fullest lips I had ever seen on such a petite face. They stood out. Damn, they were so kissable. Her smile was bright yet modest. The picture she posted with her profile was not a full bodied one but I could tell she probably sported a thin but shapely frame. A man could just tell by looking at the face. Simone's face spoke to me; actually more than her words did. I was captivated by the expression the camera had captured in her pic. I involuntarily licked my lips as I continued to stare. Stared and studied. This could be the one. I decided to respond to her ice breaking comments with some of my own.

They read: *Hello Simone, I was intrigued by your words of welcome. I briefly browsed your profile and I have to say my interest was piqued as well. Let's skip all of the back and forth jibber-jabber and talk. I hope I don't come off too bold but I believe in connections and not beating around the proverbial bush. You can reach me at 555-222-4444. Hope to hear from you soon. Until we connect*
Kwaku

The Triangle

9 a.m. of the same morning I received a text. *Good morning, Hope you have a wonderful day and I will call you after work. Take care sweetie.*

I read it several times, made me smile wide. I had hopes, was giddy with the prospect of a new woman, of a possible new love, of a partner. That day my smile was like never before, sadly it would not last and endure with what was to come. Simone called me later that day just as she had promised and our conversation was epic. We laughed, talked politics, conversed about religion and even talked about past loves. I know. Everything you shouldn't discuss when feeling someone out for the first time, we did. It was different but refreshing. I talked to Simone for five straight hours! I couldn't believe that. I hadn't had that much to say to the opposite sex in years; nor them to me for that matter. Simone was easy to talk to though. She asked questions on the sly without seeming to pry. I liked that. She also answered my queries which I find most women try to evade. Simply put, we hit it off over the phone. I quickly set up a date and she accepted. We were all set to go out for drinks Friday night. Now the hard part began. The waiting was hard. I'm Mister Impatient.

Thursday rolled in with Simone and myself either talking or texting pretty much the whole day. After finishing up some work I decided to call her again.

"Hi Simone...before you say anything, I have an offer for you."

"An offer..."

"Yes, I told you that I dabble in the art of cooking...right"

"Please Kae, watching two episodes of Chopped every week doesn't make you a chef." She laughed at that.

I could tell she was smiling fiercely on the other end. Smiling and waiting for me to continue. "Yes well...er...um I would like for you to be the judge of my culinary prowess in person."

She paused, "What are you asking."

"Duh...can you come over for dinner tonight? I know we are supposed to meet up for drinks tomorrow night but hey, why wait.

To me there was a bit of uncomfortable silence before she responded. "Kae this so sudden...changing plans an all. We already had things set for tomorrow night."

"So what," I had interrupted her. "Let's be spontaneous. You know you want to see me as much as I want you in my presence. Why wait Simone? Besides, I got Netflix over hear too."

"Well why didn't you just say that to begin with," Simone giggled slightly. "What time shall I expect dinner to be served?"

"Be here around 7:30 sweetie. I promise to make it worth your while."

"We'll see about that Kae...we will see. I'll see you at 7:30 Chef Kae."

I grinned into the phone, "Can't wait Simone."

As soon as we disconnected I ran downstairs to the kitchen, pulled out my cookbooks and tried to decide on what to prepare. If anything, I wanted the food to be perfect. Simone was like me in many ways. She wasn't too picky but she enjoyed fine cuisine. I knew from our conversations and texts what she liked and didn't like so I chose wisely and settled on a double bacon and spinach quiche. I quickly made a shopping list and headed out. It was noon.

I was at the market twenty minutes later getting the ingredients to ensure that Simone's stomach would at least fall in love with me when a text came through from her asking what I was preparing tonight. I was going to surprise her but decided to answer her question. She definitely got excited about my choice and then asked what market I was shopping at. I thought that was odd at the time but dismissed it as her just being curious. I told her and she sent a smiley face emoji with the words: *can't wait to finally meet you.*

I was just about to respond when I crashed into another shopper by not watching where I was going. Our impact jarred loose the few items that thee shopper carried in their hands hitting the floor ruined. I quickly looked up and saw perfection staring right back at me. She stood about 5'9 easily, in flat sandals. I noticed long shapely legs connected to a lovely curvature that had me mouthing all kind of choice expletives to myself. Her eyes were gray. An eye catching gray that captured your attention and held you there...petrified. I couldn't move, couldn't think, couldn't even blink as I stood there gawking like a goddamn fool.

"Excuse you." Her voice was melodic like she grew up on an island somewhere in the Caribbean. I couldn't detect a hint of aggravation in it; more like amusement.

"Oh my God, I'm so sorry miss. I should have been paying more attention to where I was going."

"Yes, you should have been or here's a bit of advice, don't text and shop." Perfection giggled. That sound had my nature rising. She said, "Damn, I now I have to get more eggs."

Eggs? I finally noticed that I must have dislodged a carton of eggs from her person when I bumped into her and now they decorated the floor and her lovely tattooed and sandaled feet. I stared at those perfect toes covered in goo, was horrified and turned on all at the same time. I couldn't believe I wasn't getting cursed the hell out right now but she smiled at me as if to say "poor little tink-tink" and strolled off to presumably find a restroom.

I snapped out of my stupor long enough to chase perfection down. "Um...miss...let me make it up to you."

"Lisa Renee is my name and how do you plan on making this up," she asked. "Well for starters Lisa Renee, let me buy you a carton of eggs."

She fixed me with some serious sexy eyes framed by creamy mocha skin and said, "Eggs...Mister I can buy my own doggone eggs." She then looked me up and down and said, "You can do something else though."

"Anything," I replied.

Her grin was sly," Anything huh...well I've got no plans for tomorrow night. I could use a good night out."

I swallowed hard. "Are you S-serious? A drop dead gorgeous woman like you doesn't have plans. Shiid, what's your phone number Renee?"

"Lisa Renee and give me your phone, I will put it in." After handing me back my phone, she turned and strolled out of the market with countless others transfixed by the natural sway of her hips. Damn, she was sexy. Lisa Renee made me lose my train of thought momentarily. I was dreaming of what I could do to all that ass tomorrow night. Tomorrow night! Shit! Simone. I'm glad I had convinced her to come over tonight. Maybe I can get out of the drinks thing tomorrow and schedule her for Saturday if tonight goes well.

7:30 on the dot my doorbell rang. Damn, I love a woman who is prompt. I opened my door to a lovely vision of ebony delights. Simone's profile pic didn't do her any kind of justice. She was absolutely beautiful.

The Triangle

A trifle bit on the slim side for what I usually go for but there were some serious curves present on that petite frame. She welcomed me with a warm smile followed by a warmer hug. I held onto her for longer than a casual minute, digesting the heat generating between the two of us. "Well hello there Mister Kae," she said in my ear as our embrace continued.

"Um...sorry...I just...well damn Simone."

"Damn what? Are you blushing?" She giggled then.

"You are a very beautiful woman Simone." Her smile stretched across her beautiful face with my testimony.

"Thank you. You're not so bad yourself. Nice arms."

I still wore my, cursed out or at the very least shot down.

"Your place or mine lounge wear; black tank and sweats. Simone sported a simple yet elegant form fitting black dress. She stood about 5'4 but still had nice long legs or was that just an optical illusion from the fancy heels she wore.

"Come on in. Dinner will be ready shortly. Just give me a minute to get changed. The time got away from me while I was in the kitchen." I lead her to my dining room and poured her a glass of wine while she waited for my return.

"Hmmm...I like your décor," she said.

"Oh, I love art form different eras, feel free to browse my collection if you like. I shouldn't be too long."

I rushed up the stairs looking back on all that goodness. Damn, those lips though! I wanted to taste the wine from them. Maybe I would.

Dinner went well. Simone loved my cooking and complimented me often throughout. She kept me engaged with vivid eye contact and easy flowing conversation. It was as if we were old friends instead of first-time-potential lovers.

"So Kae, tell me more about the type of woman that catches your fancy."

I was barely paying attention to the actual words spilling from her mouth as I was so focused on those lovely lips. "Huh...oh...sorry I was distracted by those suck-able lips of yours." Damn, did I just say that out loud. Simone smiled at me again which brought heat to my lower region. I watched her sip her wine (her 3rd glass) and wished not for the first time that I was that glass.

She said, "Stop it. I'm serious. I'm curious to know if I fit your idea of a good woman."

"Well Simone, I like a lady. I mean a woman who is comfortable in her own skin. I want someone who isn't a stick in the mud that could enjoy a day at the ballpark as well as a night out a play. I have varied tastes, varied interests and I basically am looking for someone open minded. Is that you?"

"Well I would consider myself to be open minded to a point. I like what I like and sort of disregard the rest."

"Ok...such as?" She giggled then. "I don't know, like I don't do horror movies. I'm really not into science fiction. I love country music as well as Neo Soul R&B. I can't stand rap music. Shall I go on?"

Half of what she said was totally ignored by me. I wanted to kiss Simone, so that was all I focused on at the moment. Her beauty had the superficial me in a daze. I decided to take the conversation and our bodies into the den where we could relax on my loveseat that was built for two.

Simone kicked off her heels and got comfortable. I poured her more wine and we settled into routine conversation. She kept talking.

The Triangle

I kept advancing ever so slowly to her person. Simone seemed not to notice my advancement or she didn't mind. I was on a mission, a mission to taste those lips and make them mine for the night. She was what I call 1 touch talker. When she spoke to you she touched you. At the moment, she had her hand on my knee, and I couldn't even hope to hide the bulge that grew as a result of that hand. I saw her eyes dip to its presence then dart up quickly. She continued to talk about some country music song that she loved but I knew she had seen. I knew she knew.

I tried to make some fierce eye contact of my own with her. I had my target in my sights and told myself it was now or never. Those lips! Simone kept talking; hand on my knee, gently moving it up and down. I leaned in and...

Simone's pretty little petite hand quickly came up, obstructed my momentum with suddenness. It made a nice little barrier between her lips and mine, spoiling my intent of a monumental first kiss.

"Not so fast Kae. I don't kiss on the first date; my numero uno rule. Maybe not on the second or third date either. "

I looked down at her other hand practically resting on my crotch; was this chick serious. I quickly recovered though and pulled back, got composed. "Oh, that's cool Simone. I generally don't either but I just felt a certain vibe and chemistry between us. I apologize if I misread the situation." I couldn't hide the deflation in my voice.

"No Kae, you didn't misread anything. I am definitely feeling you. Believe me, but let's just slow things down a bit. Get to know one another before the physical becomes...if it becomes a part of things." I stared at those lips again. But there it was. She had put the clamps on anything happening tonight or if ever. I contemplated a lot in the few seconds I had after digesting her words. I was supposed to be a changed man. A man looking for substance and here it was, sexy as hell and in my face.

"I'm ok with that Simone," I lied.

The rest of the night was spent draining another bottle of wine with pretty good conversation that I actually paid attention to.

Sure, I was disappointed but the truth was Simone was great company and I enjoyed myself. I figured I had time and besides, thoughts of Lisa Renee started to cloud my mental. I thanked Simone for coming and made sure she was ok to drive and promised to see her tomorrow. Maybe.

Friday rolled in and Simone and that damn Lisa Renee stayed glued to my mind. I couldn't believe the stunt Simone pulled last night though I knew she was feeling me and she wanted to feel me. Women and their damn rules! Hell, all I wanted was a taste anyway. It's not like I was going to strip bucket naked and jump her bones. Just a little kiss, that's all I wanted. Those lips though!

I texted Simone early, told her I had an important business meeting that might extend into the evening hours, then I hit Lisa Renee with a phone call.

She answered with irritation. "Hello? Who the hell is this?"

I paused somewhat put off by her tone. "Hi Lisa Renee, it's Kwaku. The guy you met at the market yesterday.

Oh...hey there hun." Her tone softened instantly.

" Sorry... you caught me in the middle of something. Can I call you back?"

"Well...um...sure."

"Ok sweetie."

And with that our call was ended. I really didn't know what to make of what had just happened. She appeared to be so interested in getting up the day before. Maybe. I decided I would just wait and see if she returned my call. I still had Simone on standby so my prospects for tonight weren't bad. To my surprise, Lisa called back within the hour.

"Hey you," she cooed. "I have been thinking about our date tonight. How about we go check out that new Star Battle flick at the the movies?"

What...a woman who wanted to see a sci-fi flick. I couldn't believe my good fortune. "Sure," I said. " I had been waiting to go until the weekend but I would love to go with you tonight. How about we catch an early show then grab some dinner after. I know a great Italian place if you're into that."

"Tell you what, you take me to see my movie and I will cook for you afterwards. That gives us some time to get to know each other...um...better. I am more of a homebody anyway at times." Her voice had me day dreaming. I liked the way her words spilled from her mouth, liked the sway of those amble size hips as she walked as well.

I remembered that movement vividly. I said, "That's fine by me, but I'm buying the groceries. Deal?"

"Deal...I'm texting you my address now so don't be late. I can't wait to see you Kwaku."

"Ditto...Renee." I felt good about tonight. It was on and I decided I would text Simone later and make plans for tomorrow night. I would wait though, see how my date with Lisa Renee went first.

I arrived at Lisa Renee's home fifteen minutes later than the time I was expected. I did that on purpose just to see her reaction to my tardiness. I was the one with the reaction.

She came out looking like a damn goddess. Hair was perfect. It cascaded down to her shoulders, flowed like she had left the salon just minutes before. The way it framed her full beautiful face had just added to all that perfection. Lisa Renee sported a banana like skin tone, bet she was mixed with something, had to be a mutt like me. The woman was T-H-I-C-K. She wore a tight sleeveless shirt with the word SPICY written in sparkling letters across an abundant chest.

Her jeans were high-end and fitted. Looked like a layer of blue skin on one of the nicest asses I had ever seen. The heels she wore made her 5'9 at least 6'2. Damn, she was fine as hell, I waited to see if a frown would accompany all that perfection due to my late arrival but she came out, big smile in tow and greeted me with a hug and a kiss full on the lips.

"Hey Kwaku," she whispered into my ear. "Let's ride baby."

I took her hand, lead her to my passenger side and opened the door for her, taking great pleasure in staring at that apple bottom spread as she eased herself into the seat. I knew the night would a happy ending.

The date went beautifully. There was much conversation with matching flirtation the entire evening. Lisa Renee seemed to be as attracted to me as I was to her. We went back to her place for dinner where she fed me by hand and did other things without hands. The sex that followed was indescribable. We went at it like animals for hours. Her phone buzzed throughout the night and one time she actually answered with me still lodged in her insides.

I knew then that we had to be discreet about things. Renee had a complicated situation that frankly I didn't care about. She stressed to me that she wasn't looking for a man and I still wanted to date

Simone so I was fine with our little arrangement. From that day on, we got up at least once a week to hang out and let off some steam.

Six months had passed with Simone and me getting closer. We did all sorts of things together. We went on vacations to the mountains, to the beach and pretty much spent most of our free time with one another. I still hadn't had sex with Simone which was frustrating to say the least but I was having such a wonderful time with her in my life that I kept telling myself that I could wait. Besides, Lisa Renee satisfied all of my physical needs. We were becoming closer as well. I must admit that I was growing attached to her but I knew there was someone else present and she kept telling me about some crazy ex of hers that just wouldn't leave her alone. I didn't do drama but I told her that if she ever needed someone to be there for her I would be.

Renee was cool. She rarely brought any of her drama into my life and actually being around her was just as exciting as being around Simone. I knew I would eventually have to let Lisa Renee go soon though. Simone was the one for me. I had decided to pop the question and spent countless hours searching for the right ring to propose to her with. I even had Lisa Renee help with the search. She never really asked about the woman that I was seeing but as my friend, she knew that woman made me happy and so she told me she was happy for me. Truthfully, I had never met a woman like Lisa Renee and inwardly, I wondered if I was making the right decision. I loved Simone but I realized that I loved Lisa Renee as well. How in the hell did I get myself in this kind of predicament. A man made tough decisions and so I chose and had to be happy with my choice.

The night before I was going to propose to Simone, I was chilling at home alone and received a strange text from a phone number that I didn't recognize. It read simply: *Hello Kwaku, you don't know me, but we have a common interest and before you make the biggest mistake of your life, you need to be shown some things. I will be in touch soon.*

I read the mysterious text several times and was just about to call the number when my doorbell rang. I peeped through the peephole and saw a shapely silhouette standing at the door. I opened the door to shock. Simone was standing there in heels and a silk robe on and she rushed me as soon as the door opened.

"It's time Kae," she said with a certain conviction.

"Simone...what are you doing," I said with utter shock clearly present in my voice.

"What I should have done months ago," she replied.

She dropped that robe and revealed nothing but her nakedness was underneath. I had lusted over this woman for months and that image was all the prompting that I needed. I scooped her up, carried her to my bed and made love to her like never before. It was like being in heaven. We fit so well together and she was so intense as if she was sexing me for the first and last time. I knew this was my forever but I gave as well as I got and we collapsed in a sweaty heap and spooned the rest of the night. As the night stretched on into the early morning, I got up to use the bathroom and heard Simone's phone going off like crazy. Someone was trying to reach her big time but she slept through the constant notifications. I couldn't help but wonder who was trying to contact my woman at 3 in the morning. I picked up her phone but couldn't see who it was because of the lock she had on it. I was puzzled but decided that it was a conversation for a later date. Simone was a business woman, so it could be just business.

But my mind went back to the cryptic text I had received earlier in the night myself. I figured it was nothing and after this night of love making, I knew I had made the right decision and looked to my top drawer where I had placed the ring. It would wait until tomorrow.

The next day Simone left abruptly with a quick goodbye and I was left alone to plan our day and how I was going to pop the question. I had made reservations at her favorite restaurant and had secured a limo for tonight's festivities. Later on that day I had received a text from Simone telling me about a crucial business meeting and could she see me tomorrow. I told her that I understood and changed the plans and reservations for tomorrow. Easy enough fix. Then another text came in from that unknown number.

I will show you tonight Kwaku. Be ready at 10pm.

I stood there wondering who was playing with me. Could it be Lisa Renee? It just didn't fit her personality so I quickly dismissed that thought. I decided to wait and see.

9:30 pm I tried calling Simone, with no luck. I tried Lisa Renee and got her voicemail as well. I figured she was with her man or something since it was a Friday night. I was anxious and stared at the time several times. 9:45 pm my doorbell rang. I grabbed my baseball bat and opened the door to a petite very attractive lady with a latin accent.

She said, "Hello Kwaku, my name is Mina and I want you to go somewhere with me."

I stood there looking at her. This was not what I was expecting at all. "Just what is this all about ah...Mina...was it? How did you get my number or know my name?"

"I will tell you everything you want to know but I need you to see something for yourself and then we can talk. Ok..."

"Fine..." Mina drove and the mood in the car was kind of strange. She made no small talk and I was in a daze about just what was going on. I just hoped it had nothing to do with Simone and her business meeting tonight. We arrived at a very exclusive community with luxury homes and we pulled up to a huge house with an open floor plan, huge windows and high ceilings made it easy for voyeurism to take place.

"Where are we Mina?" She ignored me and led me to a window in the back of the house. A window that was like a large high definition television and there was a show on right now.

She motioned for me to take a peek. I did and for an instant I noticed two very familiar tattooed feet with the word PLEASURE on one foot and the word ME on the other spread wide. Lisa's mouth opened harshly as she screeched loudly while creaming her lover's face in the process. I looked at Mina, smiled even and said," You've made a mistake sweetie. Lisa Renee isn't my lady. We were just fuck buddies and friends." Mina's expression menaced me with my declaration. That struck me as odd.

"Fuck buddies huh Kwaku...look closer."

I obeyed her request and found that that face that was just creamed with Lisa's juices was all too familiar. Simone raised her head from between thighs that I had occupied once upon a time and kissed her way up to Lisa's lips, kissing her fiercely. I watched the obvious familiar lovers go at it like there was no tomorrow coming.

I watched as Simone held Renee's face with love and they tongue danced with one another. I watched until I could watch no more. My head down, I turned and ran back to the car followed closely by Mina.

"Why did you bring me here Mina?"

"You had to know what they were doing Kae. I knew because Lisa used to be my woman before we decided to bring Simone into the picture. That bitch took my lady and filled her head with all kinds of nonsense." My head was reeling trying to comprehend what Mina was saying. "But why did Simone get in touch with me then. She approached me...she came on to me first. She said she was looking for her partner in life. That was me damnit!"

"Kae, don't you see...you were just their sperm donor. They used you to get pregnant. They played you while you thought you were doing the playing. You were targeted after they saw your profile and picture on that website. Simone never loved you. She actually hates men. Lisa Renee was the one that was actually catching some type of feelings for you but Simone reeled her right back in.

Sorry, I just thought you needed to know before you invested even more of your time with those two. I knew about their plan because it was supposed to be the three of us but I have more morals than I guess they have. I didn't want to do that to some guy. Oh...by the way, you will never have anything to do with the children if they can help it. Their plan was to relocate after each conceived and trust me Kwaku, they have the money to do just that. They plan to disappear and raise the children in their quasi family."

I stood there floored. I understood a lot now. Meeting Lisa Renee the way I did. How we seemed to have so much in common from the jump. Simone had obviously fed her all the information she needed about me. The player had been played like a damn fool. I nodded my recognition of that fact.

Finally I said, "Let's go Mina."

"Are you going to be ok Kae?"

I took a deep breath, wiped my eyes, put a smile on my face. "So Mina, do you have any plans for the evening?"

I expected to be slapped," she said.

End?

IN HIS FEELINGS
Author JUSTIN Q YOUNG

Sitting in my car with the driver's seat slouched back; I couldn't resist looking at the face of my cell phone. Every few minutes I would get the urge to press redial, only to hear Tiara's voicemail message after the first ring. I did this because I knew at some point; she would be turning her phone on, or acting as if she had problems receiving calls.

"Hey, sorry you missed me, but please leave...."

Without having to look at the phone, I pressed the end button, cutting the rest of the voicemail message off. This only added to my fury right now as my mind raced with unimaginable thoughts. For the past twenty minutes I sat, eyes fixated on the vehicle that now was parked in the shadows.

A Buick Lacrosse, nothing spectacular, which made me even madder at the thought that she would be sneaking around with a muthafucka who wasn't even on my caliber. *Get the fuck outta here*, I thought, as I compared that car to the Jaguar XJ that I sat in, for a moment. The smoothness of the peanut-butter colored leather and the cherry-colored wood grain decorating the interior, only made me shake my head at the thought of what she was choosing.

"A fucking Buick," I mumbled. Not only did she blatantly lie to me, she was fucking sneaking around with a muthafucka who wasn't even on the same caliber as me, which was making all of this worse. I pushed redial again and waited.

Hours earlier, I wanted to spend some time with Tiara because she had been mentioning how she hadn't been feeling her normal self. She was one of the women I mainly dealt with, but trusted and cared for a little differently, so I couldn't ignore her plea. Usually, when a woman tells a man something repeatedly or in regards to her health, she is requiring some kind of attention. Well, not requiring; expecting and by having a sister, I knew all about menstrual cramps and how crucifying the pain was each month, so I wanted to be thoughtful in that regard and check up on her. Though Tiara gave me the whole stomach pains, headache and attitude drill, I felt it in my spirit to see what I could do for her.

As I pulled up to her apartment complex, you could tell it was summer by the number of teenagers who congregated on and around the mailboxes, as well as in the smaller children in the grass area. Even in the confines of my car I could hear their laughter and see the joy by the expressions on their faces. *Those were the days*, I thought as I approached a speed bump, then was stopped by a moving truck that was backing out. I was becoming impatient by the driver's inability to navigate the direction he or she was going in, but the inconvenience gave me an opportunity to notice Tiara up ahead, dressed up and cheerful, getting into a white Buick.

I rose up quickly from my seat to see if I could've been mistaken, but in my gut I knew by her hair, it was really her. As the white car pulled off, I was doing my best to make out who the driver was, but the tint on the windows and the distance between both cars made it difficult. Even with the window rolled a quarter-length down, I was able to make out the blue and gold Golden State Warriors fitted hat, which immediately gave me some ill feelings.

Tiara didn't have any brothers and she didn't say any family was coming into town, so now my curiosity grew into suspicion. My heart began to race at the different thoughts I was beginning to have. Without a second thought, I whipped my vehicle around the parking

lot, causing a few bystanders to gawk in astonishment at how fast I
was going. Before heading into the direction the white Buick traveled
in, I grabbed my phone off the middle console and began calling
Tiara's phone.

I know I'm trippin, I thought, looking into the rearview mirror
periodically to make sure Chesterfield Police weren't behind me,
because of my high rate of speed and the way I was maneuvering
through the county streets. I wanted to give Tiara the benefit of the
doubt for the most part, until her voicemail came on. I looked off to
the side before trying again; feeling like just maybe she was getting a
call about the same time I might've was calling. *You making up
excuses,* I heard the inner voice in my head say. I couldn't accept that
she had lied; however when her normal phone ringing was replaced
now by her voicemail message once again, I knew this was intentional.

"Hey, sorry you missed me but please, leave a short message or
text me and I will get back with you as soon as possible."

As the white Buick increased its speed up Rt.10, from one
intersection to the next, I began feeling played by her and now the
driver, who began making a series of turns and zig-zagging through
lanes. It was almost as if they knew I was following them and they
were taunting me. A couple cars back, we all approached an
intersection where the light had begun changing to yellow. Everyone
else around was beginning to brake, but the white car sped up and
crossed through the red light. Stuck behind several cars, there was
nothing that I could do but sit and watch as the Buick got smaller and
smaller in the distance, heading to what look like the highway.

"These muthafuckin' bitches nowadays have too much sense for
their own good." Reaching for my cell phone, I called Marci, Tiara's

roommate, to see if she could shed some light on where her roommate was heading.

"Hey Jayce, what's up?" she answered.

"What's good, Marci, how have you been?" I returned, trying to sound as upbeat as possible not to alert her.

"I am my usual, how about you?"

"I just got outta the gym and wanted to bring over some takeout. I've tried to call Tiara but her phone is acting up, I believe, because it's going straight to voicemail."

"You know what, Jayce; she may still be sleep because she has been having cramps really bad all day."

"Oh yeah?" By her response, I could hear the hesitation in her voice as if she was following a script and knew she was lying to help cover for her friend. The feelings you have when you know someone is lying to you makes you want to immediately confront them, call them out on their bullshit, but instead, I made a mental note of it.

"I went in to check on her a few minutes ago and she was trying to get some rest she said, so I'm staying my distance." When she laughed, I too played it off and laughed right along with her. I would've hoped that being a mutual friend, she would've acted as if she didn't know what was going on with Tiara versus lying to me, but women cover for women; no different from dudes.

"Well, let her know that I called when you get the chance?"

"Sure, no problem," Marci replied before disconnecting.

Little did she know, I was already a couple steps ahead of her, while Marci was thinking I was being fooled.

When the light changed, I did my best to speed up in the direction that I thought I saw the Buick head in, but with rush hour traffic in Chesterfield at 4:00 pm, I couldn't figure it out. One intersection after another, I glanced to see if I could see the white Buick but they could've jumped on I-95. Frustrated as hell, I gave up chasing. I pulled up into Wawa's, parked on the side of the building and sat for a moment, contemplating my next move, replaying things Tiara said. Again, I redialed her number but was unsuccessful and heard the beginning of her voicemail again.

This situation made me begin rethinking a conversation I had a week prior with my brother about the dynamics of my relationship. Jason had urged me to stop investing as much as I had been, because he felt I was doing too much and wasn't getting equal value in return. With all the women who were in my circle and at my disposal if I so chose, he encouraged me to keep my options open.

"Trust and believe, these women act like they ain't out here for everybody, but all they really want is a come-up, just like the next Negro," he had warned.

I took in what my brother said, but I could handle Tiara.

Three hours later, after giving up chase and waiting back at the apartment complex, the white Buick returned and parked at the other end of the parking lot. I could see every so often a puff of smoke escaping from the cracked window and knew that they were having a late night smoke session. In the background, my music played just loud enough not to interfere with what I was thinking or was planning to do. The tint on the windows made it hard to detect what was going on, but I could only imagine. Being a man, I knew what windows of opportunity we looked for and this moment was a classic set-up for some pussy.

Take a chick out, spend a little time eating and making her laugh, come back home to smoke and begin getting loose in the conversation to see if she would bite, the game was basic I thought over in my head.

"I should run up on they ass and scare the shit out of both of them," I contemplated, fingering the Glock 9 that rested between my legs on the seat. A conversation held between my brother and me a few weeks earlier reinforced everything that I was feeling now at the time, how you had individuals who...

"Take advantage of good people all the time. Sometimes you have to show that you just don't give a fuck like the next individual, because the majority of people are broken and that's the only language that they respect."

His words resonated as I tried looking through the tinted windows from far away; hoping some type of movement would let me know what was really going on in there. Tap. Tap. Tap.

The knocking on the window startled me as I looked up into the beam of light that was now in my face. Holding my hand up, the beam swept across my lap and over onto the passenger side of my car. It was in that moment that I saw a badge dangling from a chain around the officer's neck. The words POLICE were in bold white lettering across his vest as he motioned for me to roll my windows down.

"Fuck!" I mumbled, doing my best to keep the gun concealed and out of the officer's line of vision. Taking a quick glance over my shoulder, his partner was checking out the backseats with his flashlight. In one motion, I dropped the gun to my feet and kicked it back under the seat while reaching for the door's side panel.

"Yes sir, what's going on?"

"Good evening, we're doing a routine check in this area. Do you have any business out here tonight?"

"What do you mean?"

"I'm asking if you know anyone in this area and why you're just sitting in the car in the dark?"

"Oh yeah, I'm waiting on a friend of mine to come home so that we can go out to eat."

The other officer said something that I couldn't make out, which prompted the officer questioning me to then ask to see some identification.

"What's the problem? I'm just sitting in my car, not bothering anyone."

"Sir, please keep your hands where I can see them. We received a call earlier about some suspicious activity and we're just following up."

Opening up the driver's side door, the officer instructed me to step out of the car. With so many police brutality cases being on the news, I went ahead and complied reluctantly, knowing this was one of those cases where they were fucking with me.

"You have any drugs, alcohol or weapons on you or inside of the vehicle?"

"Nah, man."

Instructing me to turn around and place my hands on the roof of my vehicle, the officer still patted me down. The other officer then opened up the passenger side door and began searching.

"Hold up; I haven't consented to you searching my vehicle, man, this is against the law."

The police officer continued, while the one patting me down turned me around to face him.

"Hey, eyes right here," he instructed, pointing to his eyes with his two fingers.

"Identification?"

For a moment, we just stared at one another. I reached behind me into my back pocket and pulled my wallet out and was in the process of handing my license over when his partner yelled,

"We have a firearm!"

I turned to see the officer holding up the Glock I had tried to kick under the seat. "I thought you said that you didn't have any weapons," he said, sounding a little angry that I had lied. Pulling out his handcuffs, he secured my wrists.

"It's been fired recently," the second officer said, smelling the gun.

Fuck! I thought again, mad about this new situation I now found myself involved in. I hadn't fired the gun since I bought it, but there was no way I knew they would believe me.

"That's not mines, I don't know who that belongs to."

"Well, son, looks like you'll have some explaining to do."

When I looked again to see the white Buick, I noticed that it was no longer there. She left and didn't even see me or think to look in this direction. The beginning...

"Do you even know what you want...?" Tiara started.

I paused and looked at her. The car was dark, but the light illuminating off of the radio allowed me to connect with her eyes. We had sat in her car the past 30 minutes or so, just talking about life and the direction we both wanted to go in.

"...don't get me wrong, I see the passion you have to get up and go after what you want, but you can't do it all by yourself."

"You know it's hard to really find someone who is really for you. Women see the materialistic and base the depth of how far they will allow the relationship to go on that."

"I don't think that's necessarily true, I believe we all want a degree of security and that's what most women get judged for."

If Tiara could see my lips and how turned up they were, she would've had more to say. Instead, I looked away, out into the darkness of the night, allowing what she said and my own thoughts to marinate.

Relationships were hard enough to navigate through without the added pressure of someone else's unrealistic expectations. I took a deep sigh. Tiara really didn't know my story or the challenges that I've gone through to get to this point.

"You still haven't answered," she pushed.

I turned and shook my head. "You know, I really just want to find someone who has some understanding and who knows how to play her position. Someone who is a ridah and not just say it because it sounds good, but to be a ridah when a niguh is in the trenches trying to make something happen. Life isn't always easy, know what I mean, and I'm prideful as hell. I don't know how to be vulnerable, know what I mean, I'm just being honest. I'm going to need her to be patient and understand that, so when you say what do I pray for, that's what my prayers sound like."

I felt like I had released something that I had never shared before, like a weight was lifted so to speak. Tiara placed her hand on my leg and rubbed my thigh. I looked down at her and questioned myself about how soft I probably appeared. I didn't like to do this, show this type of vulnerability because I knew how people capitalized off of it when they got mad at you. Taking a deep breath, I reached and turned up Bryson Tiller's "The Sequence", sat my head back on the headrest and closed my eyes.

I was beginning to plot my next move, because I was sensing that Tiara just wanted to sit out in her driveway and talk, versus doing what I wanted and what I had driven over here for. Her lips on mine caught me off guard,

"I believe in you," she whispered, placing her hand on the side of my face. Her lips were soft, felt small against mines. She kissed me lightly with reservation, as if at any moment it would send her over the edge, so she was being cautious. I felt it all, felt her hesitation. I didn't want her to stop, so I rose up off the seat, placing my hand behind Tiara's head to reassure her that I was right here with her in this very same moment, while in the background Bryson Tiller sang, "Am I asking for too much..."

She felt good to the touch as I reached over to cup her breast, and to feel her nipples through the fabric of her shirt. I was getting turned on as my dick began waking up and inching its way down my inner thigh. Our tongues went back n' forth as we teased and probed; the music in the background was the soundtrack to what was playing out between us. Tiara pulled away for a second and tried taking a breath, but couldn't go far because of how confining the car was, and because I went straight for her neck. I didn't want to let up, didn't want to give her a moment to reconsider the feeling as she then wrapped her fingers around my head, her breathing increasing. I could see the battle she was fighting in the dark, her excitement and her crossing her legs, squeezing them tight.

Inside my head, I was smiling. I knew what I was doing, knew I was trying to get her to that point.

"Stop Jayce, we can't," she spoke, easing backwards towards her seat and away from me. I still was moving closer towards her, refusing to quit just like that, when Tiara put her hand in the middle of my chest and said, "No, I can't."

This time I knew how serious she was by her tone and just like that, everything stopped. I looked at her for a moment before easing back on my side of the car, trying to gauge if I had did something wrong and if so, what. Were we going to go in the house, is that what she wanted? I waited for an explanation while the hardness in my pants throbbed and yearned to be fed.

"Jayce, I like you, but I don't have sex just to be having sex. I need to feel like I am your only one and that we are building something together. It's just too soon for me right now."

"Damn, so you just got me all fucked up, dick harder than two bricks just to tell me no? That's crazy."

"I'm sorry, I didn't mean for it to get that far, but you felt good and every time I tried to pull back, you got more aggressive."

I didn't say anything for a moment, I was ready to go. I picked my phone up and began scrolling through my Snapchat videos, saw Cynthia's message and typed quickly, *WYD?*

"You're mad at me?"

"Nah, we're good."

"You weren't in your phone before, but now all of a sudden that we aren't having sex, you're giving me the cold shoulder."

True, I was a little disappointed, but it wasn't life or death. I put the phone down in the middle console and looked back up at her, explaining how I needed to go. When she heard that, it was as if I had slapped her. She leaned back, tilted her head to the side and just shook it.

I was gonna say something to her but right now, it was what it was. I knew she would be mad only for a second, that's just how she was. I watched as she walked up the steps to her house, switched songs, pushed start on the Jag and eased off down the road, hoping that the notification coming across my screen would be the green light that I needed to make my next move.

FOOLISH

Kisha Green

Shayla Washington had always been unlucky in love because she was a sucker for a love story. She had read about many of them in various romance novels, so she thought there was still hope. She'd recently fallen in love with a man who like a fairy tale swept her off her feet. Memories still fresh as if they were yesterday, she could still remember how she met him. She was sitting alone in a bar, listening to Goapele's "Closer" as it played softly through the speakers.

Shayla was so captivated by the singer's voice and melodic words; it had her thinking that she too was not only closer to her dreams professionally, but closer to eventually having the fairy tale love story too. Hence, she was at the bar trying to meet someone, and that was the first step.

Shayla sat there babysitting her second apple-flavored vodka and cranberry juice; in between playing with the straw, she did occasionally eat a complimentary cashew provided by the bar. Between the game of poking the ice with the straw, she rearranged the contents in her small Michael Kors replica clutch. Sitting there bored and anxious, she didn't know why she decided to torture myself yet again, for the third Friday in a row.

Meeting a man was never her problem, as she was an attractive female, it was usually the men she chose that was the issue. Growing up, Shayla's mother often told her that she didn't use the sense the good Lord gave her. Often times she had to agree, because she frequently used what was between her thighs instead of using what was between her ears.

The last relationship that Shayla had been in had ended abruptly because after three years of dating, Raheem dropped the f-bomb; he simply wanted to be friends. Rejection is a part of life and she was alright with that, but the timing was awful since she had recently moved into his condo. That was mistake number-one; she would later learn mistakes two, three and four after finding the numbers and random nude female pictures in his cell phone.

Yes, she was being sneaky, but she felt she had every reason to since Raheem decided not to come home one night. His one night turned into several nights with no communication and when he decided to physically resurface four days later, he had the nerve to be drunk. So, she did what any curious woman would do once he passed out; raided his pockets along with his cell phone looking for traces of another woman. Unfortunately, in Shayla's case, it was other women since she retrieved thirty different numbers. She entered his birthday, 13075, as his passcode for his voicemail retrieval.

Unbeknownst to her, Raheem had taken up with just about everyone in the Tri-State area. After the tenth message from a woman named Tamika, claiming she had never had multiple orgasms like she did with him, she was too through. Listening to the messages had infuriated her so much so that she couldn't bear to hear anymore.

The real icing on the cake was weeks later she went to see her gynecologist, Dr. Greenspan, for her annual pap smear and was informed that she had two, sexually transmitted diseases. That was when shit really got real and enough was enough with the bullshit and the lies. Shayla knew that if she continued with him, there would eventually be a homicide. She knew it was over but needed to get a real plan on how to leave the situation.

She only had two hundred saved in the bank and that wasn't going to be enough to properly execute her escape. Once gone, she would need somewhere to live and with limited funds, combined with a poor credit score, who would rent to her?

After many months of saving, Shayla finally moved into a studio apartment and left Raheem for good. Those months before her departure were stressful because the two barely spoke to one another and when they did actually have to engage in conversation, it was like pulling teeth. Needless to say, she was overjoyed when the property manager called with the good news that her application was approved. Knowing she could move in on the first of the month was just what the doctor ordered and the next eleven days went by so fast. The furnishings were nothing elaborate, and she often shopped at discount stores to decorate it. Even though it was not fancy, it was comfortable; most importantly, it was hers and no one could put her out or try to manipulate her because of it. Many months had passed and she wasn't even thinking about a man or dating, declaring herself a born-again virgin, since she didn't trust any man that came at her with those tired-ass pickup lines like she was the best thing since sliced bread. Shayla Washington's life was decent and respectable, working as a paralegal was enough to pay the rent and bills. Despite not having a man to call her own; she was content or at least that was what she told herself at night as she clung tightly to her body pillow like it was her man.

One day, while driving to the supermarket, Shayla heard the "Queen of Radio" telling her listeners about a new elite hangout for singles, called the Groove Lounge. The clientele that visited this new happening nightspot was the who's who of the elite, and the ultra-fabulous and famous. Technically, Shayla had no business trying to be anywhere near the club, but like everyone else; she would fake it until Shayla made it. That choice had her currently sitting there, milking the same thirteen-dollar drink for the last forty-five minutes. She could not afford to have too many at that price.

The sixty-eight dollars in her account had to last until her next payday in two weeks. She'd already decided while getting dressed that she would live off of Ramen noodles and peanut butter and jelly sandwiches until the next payday. Shayla was not convinced that she would meet the man of her dreams, but at least she was in the building. So, what if the little black dress she was wearing still had the tags on it so she could return it.

Currently sitting at the bar, she looked through her smartphone with the dumb battery for missed calls and any unanswered texts that she might have overlooked. When tall, fine and handsome sat down beside Shayla with another attractive friend, she immediately thought, *two for the price of one, huh?* Immediately, the aroma of the handsome stranger's Gucci Envy cologne intoxicated her. She tried to act as if he didn't have it going on, when in fact he did, and so did his friend. Every time she would attempt to take a sneak peek at him, he would catch her and smile, until finally he mustered up enough courage and said hello to break the obvious silence and awkward feeling. That was the day Shayla's life changed in more ways than one.

*****

Colin had been a true breath of fresh air to Shayla. He was a total gentleman who did everything to make her often wonder, where on God's green earth had he been all of her life. In her earlier dating years, she had her fair share of handsome somebodies. Was she a whore in her day? Heck no, but she did like to refer to herself as a woman with an insatiable appetite for sexy men.

To appreciate what she currently had, she had to reflect on where she had come from. She'd kissed many frogs named Doug, Tyrone,

Dwight, Kirk, Kevin, Deshaun, Jason, Kareem, Nick, Damon, Hassan, Javier, Keith, Marc, Shawn, Charles, See-Rule, and couldn't forget, kleptomaniac Stewart. "Prince" Colin was a dream come true for her and Shayla had quickly become the yin to Colin's yang. As far as she was concerned, the couple was working on forever. Little did Shayla know, Colin had other plans.

Colin was 6'2" and a hunk of man that had never let her down once. The sex with him was out of this world. Shayla never knew a man who could truly bring that much pleasure, without the assistance of the battery-operated device that her girl, Dani, was often trying to get her to purchase. He knew her body inside and out. Shayla often lay in the bed in post-orgasmic bliss, pinching herself.

Never in a million years would she have thought she'd ever be able to trust a man again, especially one she met in a bar on a Friday night no less. Shayla had broken many rules for him, but he was worth it. Hell, she broke rule number-one for going home with him that night after a three-hour conversation, and rule number-two for giving him a blow job in his Jacuzzi that night. Drake said "YOLO" so she was alright with it too, since you only live once, right? That night was one to remember. Every time she thought of that night, she blushed in delight all over again.

"Put it in my mouth!" Shayla boldly requested in between heavy panting. Colin just grinned and kept pounding away in her love canal.

"Put it in my mouth!" she insisted for a second time. Colin heard the demanding tone in her voice, but he did not like being told what to do.

"Oh shit!" she cooed. He was forcing all types of sounds and words out of her. She was talking in tongues as her muscles began to pulsate and wrap around Colin's dick, stronger than ever.

"Come here!" He grabbed her by the head and guided her to his manhood. His wet wand glistened in the moonlight that crept through the

blinds in his luxurious bedroom. Shayla was eager to please that night and smiled in glee as she hungrily placed his manhood in her mouth. It throbbed as her tongue wandered up and down the length of his shaft in a circular, playful motion. She knew that she had him where she wanted him and he was in heaven, as he enjoyed her curious tongue. This was not her first time at the rodeo. She expertly pumped the shaft of his manhood to show him that "Superhead" had nothing on her, and this night would solidify that she was all the woman he would ever need. He was pure putty in her hands as she proceeded to lick the tip with a wet and flirty tongue.

Collectively, both of their arousal meters went up several notches. Colin began to explore her clitoris, as Shayla took him deeper into her mouth. She immediately began to taste the salty pre-cum on her tongue. She looked up devilishly at Colin and swiped her tongue across the tip of his dick like a credit card and magically, the once oozing pre-cum had now disappeared.

Colin was enjoying the feeling but not wanting it to stop; he quickly stopped her from jerking his manhood and guided her perfectly manicured hand onto his sack. She then began to fondle his balls as her lips glided down his length and engulfed him yet again. First, she gagged like an amateur because she had taken too much of him too fast. His dick was big as hell, she thought, but that did not deter her from continuing to take him until she felt his manhood on her tonsils.

"Damn, baby, you doing it like that?" he asked through his own moans.

Shayla playfully grazed her teeth along his shaft, causing his whole body to tremble. She spat on his dick, and then twirled it around. While making sure that she did not neglect the tip, she started to massage it, before she once again engulfed him fully into her mouth.

Colin looked down at her. "You better not stop sucking this dick!"

She loved sucking his dick and it showed, as she repeated her pattern. She also loved the control she had over him at this particular moment. Then, without notice, she slid his dick further down her throat, for a second time, until she could feel her lips touching his balls. Colin squirmed as her lips, tongue, and throat worked on his dick. She thoroughly enjoyed driving him wild; it gave her an adrenaline rush, looking him dead in the eyes as his dick continued to fill her mouth. Whenever he screamed her name because she'd rocked his world, whether it be with her tight and juicy pussy or her mouth, it drove Shayla crazy. She swallowed to pull him in deeper; the contractions around his tip caused Colin to shout out.

"Shaaaaaaaaylaaaaaa!" he bellowed as his hips jerked in a forward motion, causing his knees to damn near buckle.

He grunted as he attempted to pull his dick from her grasp. "Fuuuuuuck, Shay, I'm about to cum!" he whispered.

Shayla didn't care what he was saying to her, it all started sounding like a foreign language. She grabbed him tighter than ever and pulled him back into her mouth, deeper than before. Once he began to pulsate inside of her mouth, she knew what was next. Colin sprayed the inner walls of her mouth.

"Aaaaaaaahhhh," he moaned.

She kept swallowing, refusing to waste a drop of the creamy liquid that coated her throat. She peered up at him, and continued to suck and swallow, until his once-erect dick was milked dry.

*****

Every time Shayla thought back to their first night together, she knew she'd made the right decision. Yeah, it had been a long time since she felt the comfort of a man, but something in her gut told her that Colin was different. Maybe it was the good dick the good dick he kept slinging that had her acting like some turned-out chick. Maybe it was the way he explored her anatomy with his tongue, like a skilled head doctor. Not to mention, not only was his manhood big, so was his pockets.

Colin Shelton worked in public relations and with a career that he enjoyed, it afforded him a lifestyle that some often envied. Sure, financially the two were on two different levels, but Colin never made Shayla feel she was any less of a person. After a year of dating, Colin suggested that Shayla move in and immediately, she was reluctant and had flashbacks of Raheem.

This time, something in her heart made her feel like the outcome in this relationship was going to be different, and before it was all said and done; she would be not only sharing a home with this man, but also his last name. How could she *really* turn down 3600 square-feet of pure luxury, when she was currently occupying something that resembled a child's bedroom?

Immediately after moving in, Shayla's life took a turn for the better. Time always seemed to be at a standstill when they were together. Shayla wanted for nothing and as Colin treated her like a queen. Showered in gifts and trips, there was nothing missing in her life as she could see. The new couple lived like a couple that you often read about in a romance novel. The final chapter for these two would include a happily ever after with children they would spoil rotten. Never once feeling smothered or that she was not good enough, Shayla Washington finally exhaled. It was like her psyche craved this certain kind of attention and Colin was the only one who could deliver it. He wasn't just her man, he was her best friend and that was something she never had before.

One afternoon in May, Shayla had made plans to go chill with her best friend, Shawnna, who had recently purchased a townhouse. The agenda included seeing the new residence and giving her a housewarming gift. The two would catch up while enjoying take out sushi and a bottle of Saki and missed episodes of *Scandal*.

Well, plans changed an hour before she was set to leave the house, when Shawnna called to cancel because her latest boo wanted some afternoon loving, so that left Shayla with no plans but to go home. Shayla knew Colin was home, since he had texted earlier to say he was going to go for a run and work out, and then shower and relax. He'd told her to take her time and have fun with her longtime friend. Unbeknownst to Shayla that was a clue she was too "in love" to see for what it truly was.

As she pulled into the driveway, she immediately noticed an unfamiliar black sedan. This was no shock because of Colin's profession; it wasn't that unusual for him to be home meeting with a potential client or existing one. Shayla had met plenty of celebrities through Colin, so it wasn't odd if Russell Simmons was sitting on their living room floor in a yoga position, or Kevin Hart talking shit about pretty boys.

Shayla put the key in the lock, opened the door and placed her handbag on the couch while she sorted through the mail that was on the nearby table. She heard some laughter coming from the back of the house. The voices she heard were coming from the workout room, so she followed them to the door. Once Shayla caught a glimpse, she wished that her eyes could un-see what they saw.

Shayla saw Colin, whom she loved with every ounce in her, riding another man like it was a damn rodeo and he was a cowboy on the weight bench. She stood there initially unsure of what had pissed her off more; that it was a man an attractive one at that or that she and Colin hadn't had sex in the weight room yet, even though they had christened every other room in the house.

Colin and his bootydoo lover were so wrapped up in each other; they didn't even notice Shayla standing there in the partially-closed door, with her jaw on the ground and eyes popping out of her head. She stood there for what seemed like an eternity as tears began to well up in her eyes. There were no words to describe her current mood, besides livid.

Shayla stood in disbelief, unable to fully comprehend that yet again she was a got damn fool in love, but this time with a homosexual. She was not a homophobe by any means. She did feel that during their "getting to know you" phase, it should have been discussed that he enjoyed taking an occasional dick in the ass from time to time. It also should have been understood that the man of her dreams was bisexual or had homosexual tendencies *before* they were intimate and damn sure before she moved into his home. Shayla had been a fool yet again, and unlucky in love.

She was disgusted at what she found out, and at the sight of seeing two naked males together. She walked away from the weight room and made her way to the bedroom. Immediately, she was appalled seeing the lubricant bottle on the dresser right beside a new box of condoms, *at least he was protecting himself,* she thought. Shayla stood there looking at her reflection in the mirror. The mascara began to run down her face, making her look a hot mess. As she reached for a tissue to blot her eyes, it felt like time was at a standstill.

How did it come to this? Shayla thought over and over. Was life so boring with her that she "allegedly" drove a heterosexual male into the arms of a homosexual? Shayla was not feeling well suddenly and could not breathe. She needed some fresh air but before that, she had questions for her lover man. Shayla walked directly in the room and it was unclear who was more startled, Colin or his boo thang.

"Oh, my God, Shayla!" Colin shrieked as he tried to retrieve his boxers off the ground. His pretty boy lover watched Shayla nervously, frozen in fear.

Foolish

"You are gonna need more than God when I finish with you!" she screamed as she marched over to Colin. Shayla was unclear of her next move, since she didn't have a weapon and had never fought a man before. That did not matter, because she just started swinging.

"I-it's not what you think," Colin replied as he dodged her initial attempted punch in the direction of his forehead.

"Oh, well then, please tell how you ended up with a dick in your ass?" Shayla asked as her fist, which Colin never saw coming, met the left side of his jaw.

"What the hell is wrong with you?" t mystery lover man asked as he jumped up to attempt to defend his man.

"Oh, you want some too, huh?" Shayla asked him as she raised her fist again.

"Hell nah," he replied, standing behind Colin.

Shayla lunged for the both of them, which mimicked from a scene out of *The Matrix* as time was moving in slow motion.

Shayla was livid and wanted Colin to feel all of the pain she was experiencing. "How the fuck could you do this?" she screamed.

"Let me explain, Shay," Colin pleaded.

Shayla was furious and did not want to hear anything he was trying to say; she just started throwing punches and kicking him with all of her strength. The goal was to hurt Colin for all of the pain she had endured over the years from *all* men.

Shayla had clearly snapped. Her gut told her to make him feel the wrath, but her mind said she needed to regain her composure. It hurt but also felt good, but not that much that she wanted to stop inflicting bodily harm on him. After a while, she finally grew tired and had finally exhausted herself and ended the assault, got up and exited the room, leaving Colin and his boo there.

Enough was enough, she thought. Shayla was feeling lost, broken and hurt and although she had no clue of what to do, she wholeheartedly felt that Colin needed to be taught a lesson. Today, he was going to learn about actions and repercussions and never hurt her or anyone else, male or female. The pain was going to end today, once and for all. Shayla head to the closet down the hall.

There, she retrieved the three-piece Louis Vuitton luggage set. She packed all of the possessions she could fit into the suitcases. Trying to make the most noise possible so that Colin's curiosity would get the best of him and make him come investigate, but he never did. *It's all good though*, she thought as she continued packing. Shayla even helped herself to the 6500 dollars in cash in the safe. She then walked out of the room to the kitchen to retrieve the lighter fluid. She had really lost it and shouldn't have even been thinking of the unthinkable, but she had to because Shayla wasn't going to be anyone's fool again.

Shayla emptied the contents of the flammable liquid from the kitchen to the living room. The house was silent, as if Colin was afraid to make a sound. With only her luggage in tow, she quickly made way to her car. Once inside, Shayla sat in silence, replaying the last thirty minutes not believing she had been duped yet again. Within minutes, she became enraged all over again and reached for her glove compartment and saw a fresh book of matches. She calmly exited her car and walked back into the house, where without a thought; she lit one of the matches and dropped it on the floor by the couch. She didn't bother to register interest in the flames that would erupt. She dropped matches in a few more places in the living room, before exiting the house for the last time. Shayla sat paralyzed in fear before starting the engine of her car. The alert came on to remind her to put on her seatbelt while the stereo speakers played Beyoncé's "Lemonade" in the background. She put the car in reverse and pulled out of the driveway as smoke began to escape the windows of her former home. This moment to her was the equivalent of how Bernadine from *Waiting To Exhale* felt when she set the car on fire that belonged to her estranged husband; only thing missing was a Newport. That day, she made a promise to herself, but also prayed to God to soften her heart that now was going to be an icebox to help guide her so that she never would be foolish again. She also prayed Colin would make it out of the house alive and not press charges.

THANK YOU FOR THE SUPPORT!

Stay In Contact With The Authors

Author Kisha Green
Facebook: Kisha Green

Author Fanita Pedleton
Facebook: Fanita Moon Pendleton
Twitter: Moon081471

Author Danielle Bigsby
FB: Author Danielle Bigsby
Twitter: Author Danielle B

Author Nisha Lane
Facebook: Nisha Lanae

Author Justin Q Young:
FB:Justin Q Young
Twitter: OfficialauthorQ

Author Jo Dee:
FB and Twitter
JoDee Sanders

Author Quintessa Tuner:
Twitter: authorquintessa
Facebook: Author Quintessa Turner

Author Platinum
Facebook: Bridget Jones
Twitter: Author_platinum

Author KL Hall
Facebook: K.L. Hall
Twitter: @authorklhall

PAINT, N' SIP
w/ JUSTIN Q YOUNG
GET A BRUSH GET A DRINK
AND LET THE FUN BEGIN.

CHOOSE EITHER
WINE GLASSES
OR
CANVASES

MATERIALS
SUPPLIED

FOR MORE INFO EMAIL:
ACCESSJUSTINYOUNG@GMAIL.COM

It's The Write Stuff

EDITING AND PROOFREADING SERVICES

Copyediting
Line Editing
Proofreading
Fact Checking
Typing Handwritten Documents Book Reviews
Review of Submissions

Services Provided by It's The Write Stuff
http://www.itsthewritestuff.com

www.ingramcontent.com/pod-product-compliance
Lightning Source LLC
Chambersburg PA
CBHW060431180626
46817CB00007B/2766